JLm

D0007499

# DIAMONDS IN THE SHADOW

# DIAMONDS IN THE SHADOW

# CAROLINE B. COONEY

WATERBROOK
PRESS

DIAMONDS IN THE SHADOW
PUBLISHED BY WATERBROOK PRESS
12265 Oracle Boulevard, Suite 200
Colorado Springs, Colorado 80921
*A division of Random House Inc.*

ISBN 978-1-4000-7423-5

This book is copublished with Delacorte Press an imprint of Random House Children's Books, a division of Random House Inc.

Library of Congress Cataloging-in-Publication Data
Cooney, Caroline B.
    Diamonds in the Shadow / Caroline B. Cooney. — 1st ed.
    p. cm.
Summary: The Finches, a Connecticut family, sponsor an African refugee family of four, all of whom have been scarred by the horrors of civil war, and who inadvertently put their benefactors in harm's way.
    [1. Refugees—Fiction. 2. Africans—United States—Fiction. 3. Civil war—
    Africa—Fiction. 4. Family life—Connecticut—Fiction. 5. Connecticut—
    Fiction] I. Title.
PZ7.C7834Di 2007
[Fic]—dc22
                                        2006027811

Printed in the United States of America
2007—First WaterBrook Press Edition

10 9 8 7 6 5 4 3 2 1

for Maximus

# CHAPTER ONE

IN AFRICA, FIVE PEOPLE GOT on a plane.

In America, twelve people attended a committee meeting at the Finches' house. This was not unusual, but Jared Finch didn't see why he was required to attend.

Like all the causes Jared's mother and father took up—raising a zillion dollars for a church addition or tutoring grown-ups who couldn't read—bringing refugees from Africa was completely not of interest to Jared.

His mother and father seemed to be avoiding his eye, and even staying on the far side of the room. Even more suspicious, when the minister finished his opening prayer, he said, "Jared and Mopsy, thank you for coming."

Everybody beamed at Jared and Mopsy. Twelve adults were grateful to have the most annoying little sister in Connecticut at their meeting? Smiling at Jared, who prided himself on being a rather annoying teenager?

"The apartment we found for our refugee family fell through," Dr. Nickerson told the committee. "We don't have a place for them to live and the four of them are arriving tomorrow."

Jared Finch could not care less where some refugee family lived.

"Drew and Kara Finch have generously volunteered to take the family in," said Dr. Nickerson.

The room applauded.

Jared stared at his parents in horror. The refugees were coming *here*?

His little sister, a mindlessly happy puppy of a kid, cried out in delight. If Mopsy had ever had an intelligent thought in her life, she kept it to herself. "Yay!" cried Mopsy. "It'll be like sleepovers every night."

Jared gagged.

"You see, Jared, we have a lovely guest suite," said his mother, as if he didn't live here and wouldn't know, "where the parents can stay and have their own bathroom."

This implied that there were kids who would not be staying in the guest suite. So they would be staying where, exactly?

"Your room and Mopsy's are so spacious, Jared darling," his mother went on. "And you each have two beds, for when your friends spend the night. And your own bathrooms! It's just perfect, isn't it?"

Jared's mother and father had volunteered *his* bedroom for a bunch of African refugees? And not even asked him? "I'm supposed to share my bedroom with some stranger?" he demanded. Jared did not share well. It had been a problem since nursery school.

Mrs. Lane, a woman Jared especially loathed, because he was fearful that Mopsy would grow up to be just like her—stout and

2

still giggling—said excitedly, "That's why your family's offer is so magnificent, Jared."

Jared figured her last name was actually Lame.

"You will guide and direct young people who would otherwise be confused and frightened by the new world in which they find themselves," cried Mrs. Lame.

She definitely had somebody else in mind. Jared did not plan to guide and direct anybody. Jared's bedroom was his fortress. It had his music, his video games, his television and his computer. It was where he made his phone calls. As for Africa, Jared knew nothing about the entire continent except what he'd seen on nature shows, where wild animals were always migrating or else eating each other. But about Africans themselves, aside from the occasional Jeep driver, TV had nothing to say. And there was always more important stuff on the news than Africa, like weather or celebrities.

Jared would be forced to hang out with some needy non-English-speaking person in clothes that didn't fit? Escort that person into his own school? Act glad? "I decline," said Jared.

"The church signed a contract, Jared," said Dr. Nickerson. "We are responsible for this family."

"*I* didn't sign anything," said Jared. "*I* don't have a responsibility."

The committee glared at Jared.

Jared glared right back. *They* weren't volunteering to share *their* bedrooms. No, they could force two handy kids to do it. "My sister and I are the only ones who actually have to do any sharing? You guys get to contribute your old furniture or worthless

3

televisions that you didn't want anyway for when these guys get their own place, but meanwhile Mopsy and I have to take them in?" He hoped to make the committee feel guilty. Everybody did look guilty but also really relieved, because of course they didn't want to share a bedroom either.

"It'll be so wonderful!" cried Mopsy, hugging herself. "Is there going to be a girl who can be my best friend?"

It was getting worse. People would expect Jared to be best friends with this person who would invade his life. "What went wrong with the rental?" asked Jared, thinking he would just kill whoever was getting the apartment, thus freeing it up again for these refugees.

"The owner's eighty-year-old grandmother, who's blind, is moving in with her caregiver."

Oh, please. That was such a lie. How many eighty-year-old blind grandmothers suddenly had to move in with their caregiver? The owners were probably remodeling so they could sell the place for a million dollars instead.

"What are we supposed to do, Jared?" asked Dr. Nickerson in his most religious voice. "Abandon four people on the sidewalk?"

They'd been abandoned anyway; that was what it meant to be a refugee. Jared opened his mouth to say so, but a movement from his father caught his eye. Dad was sagging in his chair, deaf and blind to the meeting. Having a family of refugees in the house probably wasn't his choice either; Mom had saddled him with it. He wasn't on this committee, and the last committee on which Dad had served had gone bad. His co-chairman had turned out to be a felon and a bum. But Jared had more important things to

worry about right now. "How long are these guys supposed to live here?" he demanded.

"We don't know," admitted the minister. "This is an expensive town. We're going to have trouble finding a low-cost rent for people earning minimum wage. We probably found the only place there is, and now it's gone. We'll have to look in the cities nearby—New London, New Haven. And probably in bad neighborhoods. It's a problem we didn't anticipate."

Jared never prayed, because the idea of a loving God seemed out of sync with the facts of the world. Nevertheless, Jared prayed now. Please, God, don't let there be a boy in this family. Make Mopsy do all the sharing. I can squeeze my extra twin bed into her room. I'll even move it cheerfully. "What do we know about these guys?" he said.

"Very little." Dr. Nickerson waved a single sheet of paper. He handed it to the person sitting farthest away from Jared, ensuring that Jared would be the last to know the grim truth. "That's why we've gathered here tonight. Let me introduce our representative from the Refugee Aid Society, Kirk Crick."

What kind of name was that? It sounded like a doll Mopsy would collect. And what was up with Kirk Crick that he couldn't even photocopy enough pages for everybody to have one? It didn't exactly give Jared faith in the guy's organizational skills.

"He's going to discuss the work ahead of us and some of the difficulties and joys we can expect," said the minister.

Like there could be joy with four total strangers in your house for an unknown period of time.

The guy didn't smile, which Jared appreciated, since it was easy to overdose on good cheer. Just look at Mopsy.

"I find that my name annoys people," said Kirk Crick, "but it's memorable. You can call me either one—or neither."

This worked for Jared, who hoped to have nothing to do with the man or his refugees.

Kirk Crick launched into a long, tedious description.

It seemed that the African family to be foisted off on Jared might never have been in a grocery store, never used an indoor stove or a computer, maybe never driven a car or heard of credit cards, never taken a hot shower or encountered cold weather, never seen a shopping mall. In their entire country, there was not a single ATM. There had not been reliable electricity for a decade.

"They probably can't drive," said Kirk Crick, "a problem here in suburbia. They'll be used to buses, and maybe taxis, but mostly if they have to go somewhere, they walk. Or run. Remember, they fled a civil war. They've lived in a refugee camp in Nigeria for several years, with little shelter of any kind—six thousand people in an outdoor pen."

This was an obvious exaggeration intended to make Jared feel sorry for people who were going to trespass on his life.

"The good news is that they speak English, the official language in Liberia, where native tribal languages are used mostly at home. Their accent will be difficult to understand, but they won't have difficulty understanding you.

"According to this, the parents finished eighth grade. The kids probably attended school at the refugee camp, although those schools usually have no paper, pencils or books. Sometimes no teachers either. The children are fifteen and sixteen, but we can't tell from their names whether they're boys or girls. We'll just run with it when we meet them at the airport. We weren't expecting this family to arrive for another month, so it's just great that you people are so flexible."

Nobody here has to be flexible but me, thought Jared.

Mrs. Lame suddenly decided that everybody needed coffee. Right in the middle of the guy's talk, off she went into the kitchen, which meant Jared's mom had to go with her, and then the two of them circulated, offering regular and decaf, whole milk and skim and sugar or sweetener in yellow, pink or blue packets. Brand preference was one of the million things this African family was going to have to learn. As long as Jared didn't have to do the teaching—whatever.

Kirk Crick droned on. Basically nobody except Jared even knew he was up there; certainly not Jared's parents. They were such bad listeners that Jared didn't see how they'd ever gotten through college. They multitasked to the max. When they watched television, they were also cooking, leafing through the newspaper, talking on the phone and balancing their checkbooks. Here was information that would change their lives and they were thinking about ten other things instead.

The Finches' beautiful yellow and cream family room was a huge space, with three soft, welcoming sofas and four large armchairs. As the sun went down beyond the wall of glass, people nestled into cushions and got sleepy.

"Refugees," said Kirk Crick, "have nothing, and that also means no paperwork. People racing out of villages only inches ahead of madmen with machetes or AK-47s don't pause to collect birth certificates or vaccination papers."

Mom was arranging desserts, something church ladies did well. Jared wondered what Mrs. Wall had brought, because she was a great cook.

Then he remembered. Mrs. Wall wasn't here. It was her husband, Brady, who had co-chaired the fund-raising committee with Dad. Over two years they had raised seven hundred fifty thousand dollars for the new church building. They'd had fairs, auctions, pledge campaigns, concerts and dinners. And three days earlier, the church had found out that Brady Wall had been siphoning off that money and gambling it away at Foxwoods. It wasn't just stolen. It was gone.

Jared's mom was friends with Emmy, Brady Wall's wife. Jared had a bad feeling that one day soon Emmy would be in the kitchen sobbing all over Mom. It was going to be a very crowded kitchen, since it would also be full of Africans sobbing all over Mom. Jared hoped she was up to it, because he had just decided to sign up for every school-sponsored ski trip in order to be out of town Fridays through Sundays. The less sharing, the better.

"One problem getting refugees to America is just finding seats on a plane," said Kirk Crick. "There aren't many flights. Probably something opened up very suddenly, or four other people couldn't go after all, so your four moved to the head of the line. Your family is flying to London, where they'll change planes for Kennedy

Airport. Now, you'll need subcommittees. Who will be handling medical needs and doctors?"

"Wait," said Jared. "What medical needs? Are these people planning to show up complete with typhoid and malaria?"

"No. They get checked in Africa for that stuff. But the kids can't start school until they've been inoculated for tetanus and all. Just like any other kid starting school. They'll be spending a bunch of time at the doctor's. Your family's background has been screened as well. African civil war consists of people butchering each other. Our task force makes sure you're not getting some mass murderer responsible for destroying whole villages, or a dealer in blood diamonds, or some vicious boy soldier."

"I've heard about boy soldiers," said Mr. Lane. (Jared was always surprised that anybody had married Mrs. Lane and even more surprised that such a person ever had a chance to talk.) "Ten-year-olds who chop people's arms off and walk away," explained Mr. Lane.

No kid would do that. It was the kind of hype spewed on satellite radio—anything to make the world sound even more violent than it was.

The whole idea of screening people struck Jared as useless. Being screened would be like taking an essay test where you wrote whatever your teacher wanted to hear. We're kind and gentle, the refugees would say. We didn't hurt anybody. Goodness, no. We were the victims.

"What are blood diamonds?" asked Mopsy.

"Diamonds that are mined in West Africa and used to pay for

war," said Kirk Crick. He seemed ready to expound on this, but Jared didn't care about mines. He cared about the strangers soon to be under his roof.

"If the family doesn't have any papers to start with, how does the Refugee Aid Society even know for sure who they are?" Jared asked.

"We're very, very, very careful," said Kirk Crick.

Jared was suspicious. Right in their own church they had been careful and they'd still ended up with a major-league thief on the fund-raising committee. "Is there really such a thing as a boy soldier?"

"Yes. Often when a village is attacked, the boys are out in the fields watching the cattle. So parents get caught, killed or maimed, girls get raped and killed, villages get burned to the ground, but young boys get rounded up. They're forced to use machine guns and machetes on their own neighbors."

Nice. Jared decided to e-mail everyone he'd ever met and find someone to live with until this was over. "A boy who spends the day out in some field with cows won't exactly fit in with suburban America in the twenty-first century," he pointed out.

"You have your work cut out for you," agreed Kirk Crick. "Now, your African family may not wish to discuss their past. They want to look ahead, not back. You're getting an intact family, which is unusual. Four people who struggled and suffered and now hope to put terror behind them. Your church signed on to cover housing and food for three months and to find jobs for the parents. After three months, the family is on its own. If they can't function—and that's rare, because refugees are fighters—the Society takes over."

Three months? thought Jared. *Three months?*

Nobody but Jared seemed to think this was insane.

"You are doing a good deed," said Crick.

The committee loved hearing how good and generous they were. They sat tall. They took lemon bars as well as double-chocolate brownies. Jared's dad began talking softly to one of the husbands, undoubtedly about Brady Wall, because that was now Dad's only topic of conversation. Mom was asking Mrs. Lame for her toasted almond cake recipe. The rest of the crowd was finding car keys.

Jared was the only person listening to Kirk Crick.

"In a civil war," Crick said, "there are no good guys. They're all guilty of something. You are probably not saving the innocent, because in a civil war, nobody is innocent."

Jared had never seen a refugee; the Society had seen thousands. Maybe tens of thousands. And that was the summary? *There are no good guys?*

This made the refugee scene quite exciting. Jared's roommate would have a history of fighting and killing. On the other hand . . . how much fighting and killing did Jared really want in his own bedroom?

The piece of paper describing this family finally circulated to Jared.

On it were four black-and-white photographs that had probably been grainy and unfocused to start with. After much copying or downloading, they were so blurred that the four faces hardly had features. The photos were from the shoulders up, and everybody's hair was pulled tightly back, or else cut close, and as far as Jared could tell, these guys could be anybody. These could even be four photographs of the same person. There were dates below each photo, possibly dates of birth, but they were smudged and only partially legible.

After close scrutiny, he decided that the two on top looked older. Probably the parents. The names typed under those photos (Typed! Not even done on a computer!) were Celestine Amabo and Andre Amabo. It seemed odd that they had French-sounding names. The photo in the lower left was labeled "Mattu" and the one on the lower right, "Alake." No clues how to pronounce those names or whether the people were male or female.

We are taking people under our roof for months at a stretch, thought Jared Finch. We can't read their dates of birth. We can't tell what gender they are. We can't recognize them from their photographs.

We know in advance that they are not good guys.

# CHAPTER TWO

IN LONDON, FIVE PASSENGERS CHANGED planes for New York City. The four refugees sponsored by Jared's church were seated at the front of the economy section. They did not speak to one another. They did not look at one another. They were separated from a fifth refugee by many rows. Now and then he walked down the aisle to stare at them. They did not look back.

In Connecticut, Jared awoke almost sick with knowledge: *We should not be taking these people in.*

Jared did not say this to his parents. They would think he was selfish, racist and unwilling to share a piece of toast, never mind his room and his life.

The Finches left ridiculously early for the airport. "After all," said Jared's mother, "I-95 traffic might crawl along at thirty miles an hour, and we have to cross the Whitestone Bridge, not to mention parking problems."

They were using the church van, a vehicle Dad detested because it was unwieldy and had blind spots and a lousy radio. Mom rattled on and on. She was nervous. Even Dad was nervous. Dad traveled a lot and was comfortable in any situation, so his anxiety surprised Jared. Had Dad heard those words after all—*there are no good guys?* Or was he working out the arithmetic of building a church addition without money? Jared thought the arithmetic was simple. No money, no addition.

Or maybe Dad was thinking of Brady Wall, the friend with whom he had golfed, played tennis, watched football and raised kids. Was he imagining Brady in prison? Was he hoping Brady would really suffer? Or was he worried about Brady, trying to understand and planning to forgive?

But Jared did not talk about important things with his parents. In fact, if something was important, the last people with whom he discussed it were his parents.

His sister was so bouncy with excitement she needed the seat belt to hold her down. All Mopsy had to do was breathe and she embarrassed Jared. Now she was going to embarrass him in front of a bunch of African refugees.

Jared took out his iPod.

♦

When the plane was about to land, all passengers were required to sit in their own seats, wearing their seat belts. The plane landed so smoothly that the four refugees in front knew they were on the ground only when some passengers cheered. The refugees had difficulty undoing their seat belts. The flight attendant had to help.

Even so, they were among the first passengers off the plane.

They had learned something on that first leg from Nigeria to

England: it takes a long time to empty a large plane. A person seated in the rear cannot run down the aisle and catch up to the people seated in the front. He has to wait for hundreds of passengers to file slowly out. It would be several minutes before the fifth refugee could catch up to them.

They did not discuss this. They followed the flight attendant off the plane and down a narrow sloping corridor, which they now knew would connect the plane to the terminal. They arrived in a huge room packed with people and seats, chaos and lines. And there stood a man holding a large cardboard sign that read AMABO FAMILY.

"Welcome," he said, stepping forward.

The refugees retreated. The man smiled anyway. "I'm the representative from the Refugee Aid Society. My name is George Neville. I'll be getting you through Immigration and introducing you to your sponsors. Your family is already here, parked and waiting and very excited to meet you."

The Africans looked puzzled.

George Neville did not find this unusual. The distance between Africa and New York City was not just miles. This would be a new world for the Amabos in every way; it was natural for them to be afraid.

He could not tell who was in charge. Usually in any group of refugees, one person had a little more poise, was a little more articulate, and that person took over. George Neville offered his hand for the father to shake, but the father, a shriveled, tired man in a limp zippered sweat jacket, did not take George's hand.

Mrs. Amabo—a large, striking woman wearing a high head

cloth in a vivid orange print and a floor-length wrap with a fierce geometric pattern—whispered the words on the sign: *"Amabo family."*

The teenage boy said suddenly, "We are delighted to meet you, Mr. Neville."

George was astonished. The boy's speech was beautiful, with a British accent, as if he had been at a boarding school in England, not in a refugee camp in Africa.

"I," said the boy, "am Mattu Amabo."

Mrs. Amabo looked at the passengers oozing off the plane. "Let us hurry on, Mr. Neville." Her English was remarkably different from her son's, with an accent so thick George could barely understand her. But civil war separated families. He assumed that the son had lived in some other situation, possibly even in some other country. The family was lucky to have been reunited.

Hurrying was not something Africans usually did. They did not share the American concept of rushing here and there to arrive someplace at a precise minute. "We don't have to hurry," George Neville assured her. "We have a lot of lines to wait in."

The mother pointed down the vast terminal, where the other passengers were headed. "This way?" she asked, moving forward.

George quick-stepped to stay beside her. "After such a long flight, you look very fine, Mrs. Amabo."

She did not respond. She just walked faster.

Behind George, the husband and the son cast glances over their shoulders. George did not see this. The daughter trudged along as if she were only half there or were just half a person. George did not see this either.

◆

Jared's mom had been gripping her cell phone like a revolver. When at last it rang, she nodded excitedly to let everybody know that this was *the* phone call. Then she turned gloomy. "It will be some time before our family gets through Immigration. Be patient, the man said." Kara Finch had zero patience; her major goal in life was to do everything right now. She was a great maker of lists and schedules timed to the minute—where to be when, and what to do there, or buy there, or see there, and when to get back, and who to take with you. Jared hoped these poor Africans were braced for an American woman who planned to whip them into shape in five minutes or less.

The huge waiting area had very few seats, as if saying, Keep going—get to your cars—don't stay a minute longer.

The Finches wandered around and found seats, but not next to each other. Jared was relieved, because the last thing he wanted was to end up with Mopsy, who would babble. To his surprise, he felt the family separation intensely, as if from now on, the four Finches would be strangers.

◆

Mopsy loved sitting apart from her family, because such a thing rarely happened. She was heavily supervised, from what after-school snack to have to what television show not to watch. If she played games, it was in a group with a coach. If she met friends, it was after conference calls between parents. If she went shopping, it was with somebody's mother, and even when she went next door, it was with cell phone in hand.

Mopsy had heard of girls who were mall rats and could wander around on their own. She had never known anyone allowed to do that. She had heard of parents who let some ten-year-old babysit their newborn, but where Mopsy lived, the ten-year-old still had a babysitter, over whom a hidden camera panned.

Mopsy loved this vast airport room packed with people who did not resemble anybody in Connecticut. She loved their clothes—Indian women in gleaming saris over heavy winter trousers, Arab men with turbans, Americans back from Disney World with tans and souvenirs.

She had been awake half the night thinking about the new family. It was as exciting as Christmas Eve. She hoped these poor people wouldn't have a son, who would have to live with Jared and would end up wishing he were back in Africa. Surely one of the people in those two lower photographs was a girl. What would she be like? This was a difficult year for Mopsy, because she had no best friend. Beth and Kelly had moved away, and Meghan had become best friends with Aimee instead, and Rachel was too into sports for Mopsy's taste, and Quinnie was too new to be sure of. Mopsy planned to be best friends with this new roommate.

She could not actually imagine the Africans. Everything Kirk Crick said was hard to grasp, especially how there were no good guys. Mopsy rejected that. Everybody was a good guy deep down.

Except...if so...what about Brady Wall? Was a guy who stole from his church still a good guy?

Mopsy did not like thinking about bad people who stole. She liked talking. She said to the total stranger sitting next to her, "Are you American? Are you coming or going? We're not doing either one. We're waiting. Guess who we're waiting for!"

◆

The fifth refugee was not only in the last row, he also had the window seat. He could not even stand until his row chose to move.

In his native land, he would have permitted no man to block his way. But an airplane was not anyone's native land, so he could not beat a path down the aisle and catch up to the other refugees.

In his native land, he would have been armed. But in the land of airplanes, men could not carry weapons. He was pretty sure weapons would be as easy to get in America as they had been in Africa.

Every passenger between him and the exit seemed to be old or fat or crippled or whiny. They took forever to gather their things, and then each one dawdled in the aisle.

He stared at his watch, a thing he had never owned before, because in his former life, he had controlled time. He had never measured it. It took eleven minutes to empty the massive plane.

But it was not minutes he cared about. It was days. He had thirty-nine of them.

And then for one weekend, and one weekend only, the dealer would be in New York.

This gave the fifth refugee plenty of time to learn everything he needed to know about the city. The familiar hot excitement of combat filled his heart and he barely restrained himself from kicking his way to the front.

◆

The African family was twitchy with nerves, looking this way and that.

The mother clutched the spiral-bound paperback given to everyone in her situation: *Welcome to the United States: A Guidebook for Refugees*. Many of the refugees George met had not just read it, but practically memorized it. "In the United States," they might tell George, "great value is placed on employment. Going to work and being self-sufficient are important priorities for refugees." It was a good sign that Mrs. Amabo was reading the manual.

George collected the family's paperwork from Mrs. Amabo, and repeated their names as he checked each batch. "Andre."

The father nodded. George had hardly expected refugees to have luggage, but the father carried nothing whatsoever. His hands were jammed in the pockets of a long-sleeved, hooded sweatshirt, an odd choice for a man coming from such a hot country. On the other hand, it was January, and it must have been cold in England, and perhaps he'd been given the jacket there.

Mattu had already identified himself. The only one with

carry-ons, he cradled two small gray cardboard cartons. He was tall and lean, like a starved marathon runner. His jeans were too short, his loafers did not match and his T-shirt was too small. For the first time, George noticed a long thin scar running down the boy's cheek. "Mattu, what happened?"

"Machete," said the boy dismissively.

Mattu must literally have escaped death by a fraction of an inch. George Neville imagined him running, perhaps trying to save the sister standing so dismally beside him, or little ones who hadn't made it after all.

"Then you must be Alake," he said to the daughter.

She wore yellow cotton trousers and a faded cotton T-shirt over a painfully thin body. Her hair was a soiled nest of tangle and knot. George would have expected finely worked braids, because usually the whole camp came through for their successful ones, the ones who got to leave, and somebody would have braided this girl's hair. But in her slumped bones and blank face, George could read all the trauma of civil war. He was not surprised when she did not respond to her name.

George led them to Passport Control. The line was long and moving slowly.

The family remained silent. Most refugees whispered nervously in their own language to reassure each other, and huddled close, fearful of separation. But the Amabos did not even seem aware of each other.

The teenage boy, who was last in their little group, seemed to come to a decision. He straightened his shoulders, took a deep breath, set his two boxes on the floor and studied them. Then he turned his back on his two boxes.

The people behind him in line did not close the gap. They stared down at the boxes. Mattu Amabo had not actually abandoned his luggage, a thing forbidden in airports. But he looked as if he planned to. Armed guards were there in a moment. "These are yours?" they said sharply. They were polite, but George knew the kid would be terrified. Where Mattu came from, armed guards killed you.

Visibly trembling, Mattu picked his boxes back up, but in his anxiety, he dropped one. It fell only a few inches, but one corner was dented. A little bit of white dust wafted out.

The guards waved people away. They drew back speedily. There was never a time anyone wanted to be around unknown white dust.

George Neville's heart sank. There couldn't possibly be anything dangerous in those boxes. Mattu would have taken them through checkpoints in two other airports before he landed in New York.

Mattu's explanation was swift and heartbreaking. "The ashes of my grandparents are in my boxes," he said softly. He looked down at the container in his right hand. "My grandmother is in this one." He nodded at the container in his left. "My grandfather is in this one."

George had not known that cremation was practiced in West Africa. It was amazing that the kid had been able to keep track of his *grandparents* during the war years, let alone their ashes. George

22

was awestruck by Mattu's determination. This kid meant to bury his grandparents in this new world, where he could honor them, and keep their names alive for his own children, and their children. So the Amabos were stubborn, a great trait in immigrants. Maybe that would save them.

He glanced at Mr. and Mrs. Amabo. They were not looking at the boxes, but out over the great hall into which passengers were pouring.

"The boxes are not sealed," said Mattu. "You are welcome to look inside. But precious ash might blow out when the lids are open."

Ashes were treated by airlines as ordinary carry-ons, which always struck George as creepy. People rarely checked ashes in their luggage. No one wanted to risk losing the remains of a loved one.

The guards were skeptical. "Why did you set them down?"

"My arms are tired." This sounded fine until both Mattu and his father looked compulsively over their shoulders, biting their lips and breathing hard. The guards pulled the family out of line and led them on a circuitous route to an X-ray facility where the contents of the boxes could be double-checked.

George tried to comfort the Amabos. "It's all right. This is just a security measure. No big deal. You probably went through X-rays twice already on this trip. You're old hands now."

The boy reluctantly set his boxes on the conveyor belt. The staff finally coaxed Mattu to walk on through, promising that the ashes would arrive safely on the other side. They paused the conveyor belt to study the contents. "The bones aren't completely baked to ash," commented one.

George Neville's own parents had been cremated, so he had dealt with ashes. Even the hottest fire didn't reduce everything, and bone bits were always left. He remembered the horror of accidentally rattling his father's bones in their cremation container.

And a refugee camp would hardly feature a modern facility. They probably cooked the grandparents' bodies over an open fire, thought George, cringing. He imagined this poor brave kid collecting the ashes.

The techs opened each box and peeked in. One stuck his gloved hand down into the ashes and felt around, but the other glared at him. "Enough already!" he said, closing the boxes and handing them to Mattu, who held them with his elbows out so nobody could bump his precious burden.

But the episode was not over. The guards were now bothered by Mr. Amabo, whose attitude and posture were peculiar. "You walk through, too, sir. Take off your jacket first."

Mrs. Amabo interfered. "He keeps his jacket on," she said firmly.

"Sorry, ma'am. It has to come off."

"I'll get it," said George quickly.

"No, you stay where you are," said the guard. He frowned. The father's sleeves were safety-pinned to the pockets.

Mrs. Amabo said quietly, "His hands were cut off by the enemy."

George Neville gasped. He had not known about this disability.

He was amazed that the Refugee Aid Society had accepted Mr. Amabo. In their program, the adults had to be able to work—they couldn't show up in America just to go on welfare. The sponsors—a church in Connecticut—would have a job lined up for Mr. Amabo, and the job would require hands because every job required hands.

This guy was going to have serious medical bills. The Society would never take on such an expensive person. And if they did, they'd let the sponsor know, because sponsors had the right to refuse a refugee—if, say, they wanted a family with kids, and found they were getting four unrelated single men in their teens.

No wonder the wife's hurrying, thought George. She's scared I'll send them back.

The guard unzipped Mr. Amabo's jacket and gently removed it. Underneath, the husband wore a short-sleeved African print shirt, pressed and buttoned. One arm stopped just below the elbow and the other just above the wrist. The stubs had healed into rippled red scar tissue. They were horrifying to look at.

Mr. and Mrs. Amabo went by turns through the X-ray. The guard handed the sweat jacket to the wife, who put it back on her husband, neatly tucking the sleeves into the pockets and fastening the safety pins. The daughter, in the way of embarrassed teenagers everywhere, pretended this was not happening. Staring at the floor, she remained motionless until George gave her a tiny push to get her to walk through the X-ray.

This family really worried George.

Almost anybody in a displaced persons camp could meet the first condition of being declared a refugee: if they went home again, they'd be persecuted—which in Africa usually meant slaughtered. But to resettle permanently in the United States, refugees had to be able to thrive. George saw little indication that these people could thrive. And in this situation the refugee family was not going to be housed in a separate apartment. These guys were actually going to live in the home of their sponsor—which meant *two* families had to thrive, because American sponsors did best when they became friends with their families. The Amabos did not have an ounce of cheer or energy, the two attributes that counted with Americans. Out of all the thousands of refugee families desperate to be saved, how had these four gotten seats on a plane?

Bribery, he supposed. A way of life in Africa.

George understood. If his kids were trapped in war and famine, and he had a chance to get them out, he'd pay anybody anything.

George had never sent a refugee back. He didn't want to start now. He had a queasy moment of post-9/11 rage at immigration officers who had let nineteen killers into the country. But the Amabos weren't dangerous. They were defeated.

Wasn't that what America was about? Giving people a chance to recover? And perhaps George was being unfair to the silent, sluggish girl; perhaps she was actually behaving well, having been raised in a world where speech and action belonged to her elders.

At last the X-ray detour was over. The guards seemed a little embarrassed to have raised so much commotion over the ashes of grandparents. They escorted the Amabos and George back to Passport Control.

Mr. Amabo's eyes ceaselessly scoured the hundreds of people inching forward in the long lines. He and his wife were visibly afraid. It was George's job to comfort them, and he had failed.

◆

The fifth refugee was the last passenger off the plane. His eyes raked the crowd. The other four refugees were nowhere to be seen. It had never occurred to him that they might get separated. Disbelief turned to rage.

The fifth refugee could read but had not used this skill in years. He did not glance at some woman holding a sign until the woman actually dared pluck at his sleeve. "Are you Victor?" she said, beaming. "I'm here to escort you to your next flight."

He stared at her. "I do not take another plane. I stay here. New York City."

"No. According to your paperwork, you're headed for Texas."

The woman actually took his arm. He could not imagine a situation where he would allow a woman to lead. He shook her off. "I go with the Amabo family who got off this plane ahead of me," he said, raising his voice to make her understand.

The vast space was suddenly less full of passengers and more full of men and women in uniform, standing in the bored but grim way of soldiers. They began drifting toward him and he had visions of being turned back to Africa. He of all people could never go back.

The woman walked Victor to another gate. One of the soldiers ambled along next to him. Victor could easily overpower

one man, and take his weapon, but there were other soldiers all around. And he did not know this building, or how to get out of it, or the landscape around it. Most important of all, he did not know where the Amabo family was.

The fury that always seethed inside Victor increased. He yearned to wrap his hands around the woman's throat or around the barrel of that gun.

This could not be happening.

They could not be forcing him to leave New York. He had to be here!

But neither could he attract more attention.

Victor was helpless, a thing that had not happened to him in many years.

People would pay for this.

♦

At the final check, Mrs. Amabo held out a fat packet of refugee paperwork. Immigration went through each page. Photographs were studied. Questions were asked.

Mr. Amabo said nothing. The girl said nothing. The boy clutched his ashes.

George said a silent prayer for the Finch family. They were going to need all the help they could get.

The immigration officer straightened up the papers and slid them back into their envelope. Then he smiled at Mrs. Amabo. "Welcome to America."

# CHAPTER THREE

THINGS WENT WRONG FROM THE start.

Jared's mother routinely took hundreds of photographs, which she e-mailed to everybody whether they cared about the Finch family or not. She loved to chronicle her children's lives. Jared figured half the reason Mom wanted to host a refugee family was to start a new scrapbook, plus flood the church Web site with a million photos.

The four Africans had assembled on the sidewalk on the departure level. They stood with their backs to each other, wild creatures keeping watch in every direction. They were so fearful that their eyes flared open, as if they were gazelles scenting a predator.

I'm comparing these people to animals, thought Jared.

The mother was statuesque in her colorful wrappings, while the father was bent and cringing in a faded sweatshirt. There *was* a son—Jared's age, lanky and athletic, with extraordinarily black skin. The daughter, much lighter in complexion, was deathly thin, her hair wild as jungle vines.

Mom lifted her digital camera.

The African mother raised her hands in the universal gesture for "No!" and repositioned her family until they were too far apart to be in one shot. "No photographs," she ordered. Her accent was thick and soupy; and if she had not been pointing at the camera, Jared would not have figured out the word "photographs."

"It's for the scrapbook!" cried Jared's mother, speaking clearly so they would grasp the importance of her hobby.

Jared wanted to fall through the sidewalk. Like Africans cared whether Kara Finch kept a scrapbook. These people had been trying to stay alive, not position photos on a page.

"Great," whispered his dad. "We haven't even said hello yet and we've already tripped over some tribal taboo."

Maybe a hundred years earlier. Even twenty. But in the television, Internet, digital-camera era? Jared doubted it.

His mom flushed and dropped the camera into her purse.

The African mother was equally embarrassed. She bowed slightly, and then they all bowed, as if it were suddenly 1800 and the Finches were used to bowing. Mom recovered. Throwing her arms around this large, impressive African woman, Jared's mother said, "I'm sorry about the camera. I'm Kara Finch and you're part of our family now. You'll be living with us. Welcome to America."

The woman was shocked. "Living with you?"

"I know you expected your own apartment, but that didn't work out after all. We'll have lots of adjustments to make," said Jared's mother happily, because she loved adjusting, whereas everybody else hated it and wanted everything to stay the same. "I know we'll be best best friends."

The Africans were stunned by this conviction.

So was Jared.

"Thank you," said the African mother dubiously. "I am . . . Celestine Amabo, and I am happy to be in your country." She did not look happy. She was breathing fast and shivering.

Dad, meanwhile, was trying to shake hands with the father, but the man kept bowing instead. "I am Andre," he said. "I thank you because you take us in. God be with you."

My turn, thought Jared, who totally did not want a turn. He faced his future roommate. "I'm Jared," he said reluctantly.

The boy was taller than Jared, willowy and hard, like men who win marathons. Handsome. Hair trimmed so short it was hardly there. He held two containers that didn't look as strong as cereal boxes.

"I am Mattu," said the boy. He hardly glanced at Jared, his gaze still swinging in all directions. How could he have such huge eyes? Wasn't eye size pretty regular among human beings?

"If he's Mattu," Mopsy cried, "then you're Alake! Am I saying it right? A lake? Is that who you are? I'm Mopsy! You're going to share my bedroom! We'll have the best time. I love sleepovers. We've got all new sheets and blankets for you!"

The African girl didn't even see Mopsy, let alone hear her—a skill Jared would have loved to possess. He had the awful thought that the girl was blind.

Dad's hand still hung in the air. He was staring at Andre's sleeves. The wind flattened them.

"He has no hands," said the mother softly. "The rebels chopped them off."

That little detail had not shown up in the grainy, above-the-shoulders black-and-white photo. Since they'd had no idea what skills, if any, the adults would have, Jared's dad had gone ahead and found work for Andre at the Quick Lube, vacuuming cars, on the theory that anybody could manage that.

Wrong.

The refugee officer was just standing there, looking worried. Yeah, thought Jared, I'd say sponsoring a guy without hands is something to worry about.

Repositioning his boxes, Mattu extended his right hand for Jared to shake. His grip was firm. Jared tried to imagine life— Andre's life—without any grip.

"Andre, how terrible!" cried Mopsy. "It must have hurt so much! Does it still hurt? Who would do that, anyway?"

Jared would have said a guy without hands had nothing to smile about, but Andre Amabo smiled at Mopsy. "In a civil war," he said gently, "people forget that they are people. Next they forget anyone else is a person. They forget how to be kind. They learn to hurt. In our wars, they might execute you, but usually they chop hands off, so that you suffer before you die. If you live, you are helpless and must depend on others."

"You can depend on me," promised Mopsy.

It had never crossed Jared's mind that the Africans would actually converse, and certainly not about important things like suffering. I'm a total racist, he thought. I figured they'd have a ten-word vocabulary: "car," "shoe," "food."

Since Mopsy couldn't take Andre's hand, she took Celestine's, as affectionately as if this African woman had already become her favorite aunt. "The Refugee Aid speaker *told* us there are no good guys. This is what he meant!" said Mopsy, hanging on to Celestine and pointing to Andre's sleeves. "But why didn't you bleed to death, Andre?"

"I ran away with my arms up in the air, to try to stave off that fate. When I got into the bush, I found my wife and she bound up my wounds."

Andre's pronunciation was not easy to follow. Jared had to decipher the words, say them correctly in his head and then dope out the meaning.

"What kind of bush is big enough to hide in?" Mopsy asked.

" 'Bush,' " said Andre, "is our word for . . ."

"Wild places," supplied Mattu.

"Is that when you got your scar, Mattu?" said Mopsy, who would ask anybody anything. "What happened? Who attacked you?"

◆

Mattu could not get his bearings. There seemed no way to depart from these four people named Finch. Mattu had known that a counselor would be here to explain things. But a mother and a father? A son and a daughter?

He had expected to walk off the plane and be beneath the famous skyline: the tall, jagged profile of Manhattan. If such a place was nearby, he could not see it. How could he lose himself in the city of New York when New York did not seem to be here?

They were standing outdoors, yet there was no outdoors. There was a forest of buildings and roads and churning traffic. Hundreds of people scurried by and vanished. Mattu tried to focus on the bouncy, bubbly little girl. "It's from a machete."

"Oh. What's a machete?"

A person her age did not know what a machete was?

Mattu tried to figure that out, but it was difficult to think about anything except that the fifth refugee had not caught up to them. Victor must still be in one of the lines. Perhaps his paperwork was not acceptable. Perhaps they were not telling Victor "Welcome to America." Mattu could not imagine being so lucky. Any moment now, Victor would come hurtling toward them.

*But what if he didn't?*

"Everybody's shivering," said the American woman. "Let's pile into the van, turn up the heat and get going." She began to herd them toward a large white vehicle.

Mattu and Celestine looked at each other for a long moment.

Mattu considered the Refugee Aid Society officer. It was dangerous to trust anyone. But Mattu had no other source of information. Very softly, Mattu said to George Neville, "The other refugee on the plane does not come with us?"

"Oh, right, I was chatting with the woman meeting him. She's with some other service. Refugees get distributed all over America, you know. Wherever there's a sponsor. She was flying him to another destination. Texas, I think. Is he a relative? I can try to track him down."

"He is a stranger," said Mattu. "I did not realize he would go to another place. It does not matter. Thank you for your kind assistance, sir."

Victor had killed to get here.

And now he had not gotten here after all.

♦

The African mother touched the edge of the sliding door, peered inside the van and then looked nervously back at the airport. Mr. Amabo wet his lips and studied his feet. Mattu balanced on the curb.

They're afraid to come with us, thought Jared.

How weird to think of his family as frightening.

Jared's practical mother interpreted the hesitation differently. "Shall we all go to the bathroom again before we take off?"

Celestine Amabo seemed to come to an important decision—the decision, perhaps, to trust his mother. What incredible trust in the future it must have taken to get on a plane at all, to leave an entire continent and everything they knew.

"No, thank you," Celestine told Mom, and she climbed into the van. Andre lurched in after her. They took the second row of seats, right behind Jared's mom and dad. Mattu followed, bending like a straw in a juice box, carefully managing his ashes. He chose the far rear corner, slumping, as if he didn't want to be seen in a church vehicle.

Alake—whose name they did not yet know how to pronounce—was still on the sidewalk. Her parents didn't look to see if she got in, never mind if she was happy about it. Mopsy shoveled her into the van and pushed her down in the third bank of seats so that Alake was against the window right in front of Mattu, while Mopsy sat in front of Jared.

How different was the bone structure on each African face. Andre and Celestine had broad, solid features, while Alake's face was thin and bony, and Mattu looked like a statue of some ancient Greek god, carved from ebony instead of marble.

Dad turned the heat on high. It was warm for January, about forty-five. But if you lived near the equator, you were probably used to a temperature twice that. More than.

The van seated twelve and was therefore nearly useless to the church, because even the smallest youth group had thirty kids. But today it was roomy: four Amabos and four Finches. No other committee members had come because everybody assumed suit-cases would fill the extra space.

How American, thought Jared, to expect refugees to have luggage. "So what's in the boxes, Mattu?"

◆

Mopsy was happy. There was a girl.

Too old for middle school, but that was Mopsy's fault; she had neglected to explain to God that the sister should be her own age. It seemed to Mopsy that an all-powerful God should be aware of these details on His own, and she was irked, as she so often was, that God needed all this nagging.

Mopsy studied the girl eagerly. Right in her backyard, she must have had elephants and lions and a hippo or two. Mopsy could hardly wait to hear what it was like to live in the middle of a safari. The girl had lovely skin, coffee with milk; she was a completely different color than her parents, who were brown, or her brother, who was black. To look at them, you would never know these four were related. Of course, you would never know Mopsy and Jared were related either, because he was large boned and dark haired, while she was small boned and blond; his eyebrows were heavy and frowning while hers were invisible over pale blue eyes.

Mopsy had planned to get rid of her nickname when she started fourth grade, but nobody had cooperated. She had tried again in fifth and failed, and now in sixth grade was once more trying to be Martha, but everybody still said Mopsy. She said to her new sister, "My name is Martha. No matter what anybody else calls me, Alake, you say Martha."

Alake did not look at Mopsy. She didn't look out the window either. As far as Mopsy could tell, she didn't look, period. "Alake? Can you hear me?"

Alake did not move.

Mopsy leaned forward and tapped Celestine on the shoulder. "Can Alake talk?"

"She lost her speech," said Celestine, as casually as if Alake had lost her sunglasses.

Mopsy's heart broke for Alake. What could be worse than not being able to talk to your friends?

"We'll get her into therapy," said Mopsy's mother from the

front seat. "When Alake sees that she's safe, she'll begin talking again."

Mopsy's school had battalions of people poised for situations like this. There were counselors and special-ed people, speech therapists and a music therapist, interpreters for the hearing impaired, tutors and referrals to doctors.

Mom began shouting directions to Dad, who loved everything about his wife except her tendency to give driving instruction, and of course he wouldn't do what she said, and of course she was right, so Dad missed the airport exit and Jared heaved a sigh while Mopsy giggled and Mom said, "Really, Drew," and Dad said, "Kara, just let me do this," and they went all the way around a second time.

Celestine's marvelous head wrap was crushed by the van ceiling, so she took it off. Her hair was glorious—intricately braided and beaded. What a contrast to Alake's hair, which looked as if it hadn't been fixed since the family's escape into the bush. Who didn't want nice hair? Maybe Alake wasn't talking because her hair embarrassed her.

Mopsy squeezed Alake's hand to let her know that Mopsy was her friend, but Alake did not squeeze back. Mopsy called up to the front seat, "You know what, Mom? Alake should come to sixth grade with me, even if she is fifteen. She might as well not talk sitting next to me. My friends are nice, whereas Jared doesn't even have any friends, and if he did they wouldn't be nice."

"Excuse me?" said Jared.

"I think that's a wonderful idea, Mopsy," said Mom.

"*Martha,*" she corrected.

Mattu said to Jared, "Aren't mops for cleaning floors?"

Jared laughed.

"We didn't mean to call her Mopsy," said Mom. "It just happened. 'Mopsy' is sort of from the word 'moppet,' which means rag doll."

"Which leads to 'Muppet,'" said Jared. "Half puppet, half moppet. Like *Sesame Street.*"

"Is that where you live?" asked Mattu. "Do you grow the seed, the sesame?"

The van was silent. The Americans began to see just how much the Africans did not know.

Dad gave the whole sesame seed thing a pass. "We've left Kennedy Airport, and it hasn't been easy, since I kept missing the exit lane. But we are now on the highway and headed home."

Mom swept her four guests with her wonderful smile. "You're here! You're really here. You made it!"

Tears slid down Celestine's face. Andre smiled tenderly at his wife and wiped them away. Not with his hand, because he didn't have one, but with the knob of his arm, hidden under the sleeve. Mopsy kind of wanted to see the chopped-off part and kind of didn't.

"Seat belts," Mom reminded everybody.

Celestine reached around to fasten Andre's seat belt. Mopsy had an awful thought. If Andre's *arms* had been cut off, maybe Alake's *tongue*—

Mopsy decided not to go there.

Since Alake's hands lay in her lap as if they had been sewn down, Mopsy fixed Alake's seat belt. Alake did not react to having this white person lean over and cinch her in. I will save her, thought Mopsy. I will make everything better. She took Alake's cinnamon-colored fingers and curled them around her own.

Celestine said proudly, "This is the third time I have worn a seat belt."

Mopsy and Jared exchanged looks, a rare event. They were always peeved on planes when the flight attendant wasted time describing how to snap the seat belt halves together when every single person on earth already knew.

Wrong.

♦

Mattu did not seem to hear Jared's question about the boxes. "Are we close to the home in which you live?" he asked.

He had a sort of British library voice. What with that and his marathon-runner build and good looks, Jared bet every girl in high school would have a crush on Mattu by the end of the first week. "Nope. We have a three-hour drive. You landed in New York, but we actually live in the state of Connecticut."

Mattu repeated the sentence carefully. "We actually live in the state of Connecticut." His English was accurate and clear, a contrast with Celestine's muddy accent. It seemed odd that the son had a different accent from the parents.

The speechless girl was pretending to sleep, leaning against the window to keep Mopsy at bay. Then Jared remembered how long she'd been on the road. She wasn't pretending. She'd collapsed.

Mom was explaining the joy of scrapbooks to Celestine. "We want to document everything, because the church is so excited to have you. I'll make a souvenir book for you too, of course, and one day we'll look back and see exactly what it was like on the first day, and what we wore, and we'll share pictures with everybody and you can send them to friends already in America or friends you left behind."

"We beg your pardon," said Andre. "We will be grateful to be part of a church again. But no pictures."

It was now hot in the van. Andre shrugged off his jacket. Jared could see one of the stumps. He had never seen an amputation. The violence of what had happened to Andre was visible right there on the rough, scarred stump.

Jared's mom tended to ignore opinions that were not hers. "We'll get you a cell phone. You can send photographs through your phone, you know."

"I have never used a phone," said Celestine.

Mopsy and Jared shared their second look. Somebody existed on earth who had never used a phone?

Mom whipped out her cell to give a lesson. Three out of four Africans leaned forward to learn. The speechless daughter, no surprise, wasn't interested in telephones. Jared took out his own cell to show Mattu what Mom was talking about. Jared called his mother in the front seat and three Africans burst into laughter when Mom and Jared chatted across the space of two car seats.

Jared photographed Mattu with his camera. Mattu saw his picture in the tiny phone and laughed delightedly.

"I can send this picture of you over the phone," explained Jared, "or bring it up and look at it when I feel like it, or transfer it to my computer and print it out or send it to anyone in the world."

Mattu's pleasure vanished. "Send it?" he repeated. The concept seemed to worry him. "Can it be made to disappear wholly?"

"Sure." Jared deleted it. Mattu didn't relax. Jared shut the phone and put it in his pocket. Now Mattu relaxed.

He's not afraid of the photograph itself, thought Jared. He doesn't want a photograph *to exist*.

Come on. I have seriously been watching too much television.

◆

The bouncy, bubbly American girl reminded Alake of her sister, except a different color. Alake had rarely seen people the color of these Americans. But people of any color meant little to her. Only the dream had meaning.

For a long time, Alake's sleep had been as light as gauze, protecting her from nothing. Inside the frail netting of this sleep was the dream, always the same dream. Alake slept, her head against the window of the van. Perhaps Mopsy's mention of sixth grade made the events in the dream start earlier than usual, because Alake too had been in sixth grade when it happened.

In the dream, Alake could hear laughter. There had been twenty-nine relatives living in her compound, and their servants, and various friends who had come to stay, and children who had been orphaned. Had they been happy enough to laugh on that day?

Alake and her sister had not yet left for school. Alake didn't know why that was. Her parents cared deeply about education, and the children were never allowed to be late or to miss a day of class. Perhaps her parents had known something was about to go wrong; perhaps they had been preparing to run but had begun too late. But then why were they laughing?

A voice pierced Alake's dream. "Look!" cried the American mother. "On your left! The skyline of New York!"

Alake woke. But she did not look. She did not know how to look anymore.

♦

Mattu looked.

New York was exquisitely beautiful, outlined against a brilliant blue sky—and very far away. The van raced on. New York was already gone.

Mattu had experienced traffic. But there were more cars and trucks on this road than he had known existed in the world. They came at the van with such ferocity that he expected constant collisions. After a while he grasped that there was a cement wall between the van and the oncoming cars. The road also had side walls so that you could not just drive off. Mattu tried to estimate the distance of the walk back to New York. He had not yet seen anybody walking. In fact, there were no paths.

Throughout this fearsome trip, the boy and the girl peppered him with questions. Mattu envied Alake, who had already established that she wasn't answering. "It is difficult to speak of the past," he kept saying.

The American boy talked of school.

Mattu had expected to hunt for a job, because that was the instruction in the manual that he and Celestine had taken turns reading during the long hours of flight: a job was the most important thing and must be gotten right away or Americans would lose respect for you. He had no idea what kind of job he could do and could not picture how he would live—what sort of building he'd live in; what sort of food he'd eat. It had not occurred to him that instead of working, he might be allowed to attend school. Jared's descriptions were intoxicating. Books and learning, teachers and computers, sports and friends, food and games. Jared had a used laptop that would now be Mattu's.

Mattu knew what computers were, but he had never touched one. He knew what a lap was, but not what it had to do with computers. He tried not to ask, because the answer would be too tempting, and he must not be tempted; he had another assignment to complete; but he said, "What is a laptop?"

Mattu drank in Jared's words. He, Mattu, now owned this? The American boy described an amazing bedroom in which they would have their own television and movies and music. Mattu could not help asking more about the school and the bedroom.

A police car raced by, siren shrieking and lights whirling. Jared did not even notice. Mattu could not fathom being so unaware of armed men. He prayed for the person they planned to kill.

The ride went on and on, the little girl demanding answers and Andre and Celestine responding.

The American father, Drew, cleared his throat. "Now, I know you all expected a place of your own, and we expected that too, but it didn't work out. For the first few weeks, you'll be living with us."

The American mother, Kara, beamed, which seemed to be her usual manner. "Celestine and Andre, you will have your own bedroom and bath. Mattu, you'll share Jared's room and bath, and Alake, you'll share Mopsy's. We'll cook meals together and learn how to run a household together. I think in the end we'll be glad it worked out this way, because we'll get to know each other so well."

Mattu prayed that they would not, in fact, get to know each other so well.

The van left the remarkable walled road, and at last they were in America itself, among houses and people and stores. There were countless trees without leaves and lines of pretty stone walls that did not seem to enclose or achieve anything. All the roads were paved. All the houses were perfect.

Mattu tried to keep track of the route so he could get back to New York, but the van turned, waited at traffic lights, climbed hills and went over small bridges. Mattu thought: No one can find us here.

The four of them had not been interviewed, of course, but everybody knew how the Refugee Aid Society ended every session by saying, "In America, you will be safe."

Nobody believed that, but they went along with it, because they had to play their parts.

Now Mattu thought, Could it be true?

Could I be safe in America?

# CHAPTER FOUR

MOPSY COULD HARDLY WAIT TO get home. From now on, her house would be packed with people coming and going, dropping off casseroles and desserts, helping drive the Amabos wherever they needed to go and discussing unplanned stuff like Andre's failure to have hands and Alake's failure to have speech.

At last Mopsy's father drove up Prospect Hill. It was so steep and the wind at the top was so fierce that even though the town had been settled in 1660, no one had built there for centuries. Then, a few years ago, a developer put in a long switchback road, and now the hill sported eight homes with big garages and fabulous views of the waters of Long Island Sound. Instead of grass, their yards had rocks, mountain laurel and poison ivy. Mopsy reminded herself to explain poison ivy to the Africans.

Signs were tacked to a row of telephone poles: WELCOME AMABO FAMILY! WE'RE GLAD YOU'RE HERE!

Celestine and Andre read each of these aloud. Mopsy loved how surprised they were. And then, to her utter delight, not only were her driveway and yard full of friends and church family, but the local TV station had come! Everything counted more once it was on TV, and it was so fun to get credit for stuff.

But Andre cried out, "No! No pictures. I cannot get out of the van."

Mopsy's heart sank. Andre was right. TV would totally love zooming in on Andre's chopped-off arms. They'd pretend to be all compassionate and everything, but really, they'd feast on his suffering.

Dr. Nickerson came trotting over. He was a nice guy who gave short sermons, which Mopsy's father always appreciated, and he was also a runner, so you were always seeing him loping down some sidewalk. Mopsy opened the sliding door of the van. "Hi, Dr. Nickerson!" she yelled.

The Africans pressed up against the far windows as if the minister were spreading disease.

"No cameras, Pete," said Dad. "I don't know if it's a cultural thing or what."

Dr. Nickerson looked as if he had been slugged. His smile vanished and his face grew lined.

Mopsy had forgotten. This very same TV station and both of the local newspapers had gleefully covered Brady Wall's theft. They did not tire of stating that in organized religion, either priests were out there touching little boys or deacons were out there stealing donations. Poor Dr. Nickerson. This would have been some much-needed good publicity.

The minister trudged back toward the crowd, telling them

that film was offensive to the religious and tribal habits of their new guests and that sensitive people would back off.

Nobody with a camera *is* sensitive, but everybody wants to *think* they're sensitive, so finally, the TV people gave up and went away. Even Mrs. Lane left, and she did not easily go along with anything.

The Amabos sat in the van, hands—or in Andre's case, sleeves—over their faces.

Except Alake, who had not noticed.

♦

On the plane to Texas, a passenger asked to be reseated. He did not make eye contact with the fifth refugee when he moved. He considered alerting the flight attendant that there was something wrong with the man in 23B. He decided this would only delay the flight.

♦

Step one, said Mom, was the bathroom. She would take Celestine and Andre to theirs, Jared would take Mattu to his and Mopsy would take Alake to hers. Everyone must be grimy after so much travel. Everybody was to borrow a bathrobe after they took a shower, and meanwhile Mom would run everybody's clothes through the wash, since nobody had a change.

Jared ran up the stairs with Mattu carefully climbing after

him, balancing his boxes. "Where do you want to put those?" asked Jared.

Mattu was too busy staring at his new room to answer.

For all Jared knew, in Africa ten families would sleep in a room this size. Jared didn't feel like thinking about that stuff. "This is your bed," he said, pointing to the one he normally used as a table. It had been cleared off and had clean sheets. Flannel sheets, which Jared detested, but which Mom felt were cozy in winter.

Mattu continued to hold his boxes.

"What's in them?" asked Jared again.

"The ashes of my grandparents."

Jared was speechless. All four of his grandparents were alive and well and probably playing tennis or golf right now, since they wintered in Arizona. He couldn't stand thinking of his beloved grandparents disappearing into some shabby little cardboard box.

The dormer window had a large ledge, almost a seat, which Jared used as a drop-off spot for anything he might want again one day. He swept everything onto the floor and dusted the surface with the flat of his hand. Since Jared was always hot, he generally left this window cracked. A sliver of cold air shivered over the ledge. It felt good. Jared opened the window wider.

By day he had a fabulous view of the water, but Jared had no use for views. What he liked was the cliff. Jared and his friends used to play Search and Rescue up and down that cliff, but when they got older, they played soccer in the road instead. Now everybody he knew had a driver's license (except Jared, whose parents did not think he was mature enough to drive, but somehow he *was* mature enough to sponsor a refugee) and nobody hung around playing ball anymore.

Mattu set his boxes down and flexed his arms.

He must've been holding them for like twenty-four or thirty-six hours, thought Jared. He turned on the shower, showed Mattu how to get the water hotter or cooler, handed him a washcloth and towel, flung a bathrobe onto the counter and left. He had no idea whether Mattu was used to showers and flush toilets and soap that pumped out of a plastic bottle. But a guy who could hang on to his dead grandparents' ashes through a civil war, two continents and Immigration could probably manage a bath.

♦

Mopsy got Alake upstairs by pushing lightly in the middle of her back. The minute Mopsy stopped pushing, Alake came to a halt. It was a slow trip.

Mopsy's bedroom was pink, white and frilly, but her bathroom was yellow, with yellow towels and a yellow and white striped shower curtain and a yellow and green finger painting Mopsy had done in nursery school. Mopsy pulled Alake off the thick pink carpet of her bedroom and onto the white tiles of the bathroom. Alake showed no sign of knowing what a bathroom was for.

Mopsy peeled off her own clothing, hoping Alake would follow this example, but Alake didn't, so Mopsy carefully tugged at the girl's T-shirt. Alake lifted her arms, her first voluntary move, and Mopsy felt pretty good about that.

Nothing more happened.

Mopsy's shower was a square stall with a clear sliding door. She turned on the shower, checked the temperature, got in, soaped, rinsed and stepped out. She wrapped herself in a huge yellow towel. Then she pushed Alake—still half dressed—under the water and slid the door closed.

She went back into the bedroom to give Alake a little privacy. Maybe Alake would get bare under the shower. After a while Mopsy went back in the bathroom. The shower was still running, but all of Alake's clothing was now lying on the floor and she was dripping on the mat, a towel around her just the way Mopsy had done it. She looked clean and relaxed. Or maybe Mopsy was making that up.

Mopsy turned off the flow of water and held out the sleeves of her bathrobe, which was short on Alake but fleecy and warm. Mopsy tied it around Alake's waist, stuck floppy bunny slippers on her feet and tugged her downstairs.

She was pronouncing the name "a lake." It occurred to her that nobody in the African family had used the name yet.

♦

Two people could sit on stools at the kitchen bar, and eight at the farm-style table. Jared looked with satisfaction at the feast provided by the church ladies. It was sufficient for a castle during a siege, or else teenage boys.

Here at the back of the house, there was no view of anything, and with the sun down, there was nothing outside but darkness. "We must close off the night," said Celestine urgently.

"It's okay," said Mom. "There's nothing out there."

"There is always something out there," said Celestine.

They must have seen American TV news, which loved crime above all else. Celestine probably figured that what you found in an American backyard was murderers.

"That's Africa," said Mom, smiling. "This is a totally safe neighborhood. I love the dark."

Clearly the Africans considered this insane. Nobody moved toward the dinner table, because they couldn't breathe, never mind chew, with all that darkness staring at them.

Mom, who had solutions for everything, went and got sheets, which she thumbtacked over the windows.

Andre was now clad in Dad's bathrobe. It was pale gray terry cloth with elbow-length sleeves. His stubs were hideously visible, shiny and swollen and pitted. Evidently Andre didn't care about people seeing the stubs. He didn't realize that in America, anything ugly about your body, you hid or solved, whether it was buck teeth or a birthmark.

"This is like Thanksgiving," said Mopsy happily. "Although for Thanksgiving, you can't have some mountain of rice, I wonder who brought the rice, you have to have mashed potatoes. Which are better," she added, like some future Mrs. Lame, forcing everybody into her own lifestyle and choice of carbohydrate.

Dad bowed his head to say the blessing.

Jared never closed his eyes during prayers. He lost his balance if he closed his eyes. Plus it signified a degree of participation Jared refused to make. He listened but didn't pray. Alake didn't close her eyes either, but that didn't matter, since she didn't see to start with.

"Father, we thank thee for our new friends, who have arrived safe and sound."

Jared wasn't so sure. Alake did not seem sound in mind or body.

Jared's dad paused, as if wracking his brain to come up with some other blessings, and to Jared's amazement, Andre took up the prayer. "Father in heaven, we thank you that we are safely under this roof. We thank You for this fine food you have put on the table before us. You have blessed us."

Andre, who wasn't able to eat with his fingers, never mind his fork? Andre thought he was blessed?

"Dear Jesus," added Celestine, "we thank you for Drew Finch, Kara Finch, Jared and Martha, and for the minister of your church, who protected us."

There was another pause, as if people thought that somebody else—Jared, for example—would also pray. They were wrong. Finally Dad said, "Amen."

"Thank you for remembering my name is Martha," said Mopsy.

"Your name is Mopsy," said Jared. "Only mature women can be called Martha."

"Don't bicker," said their mother.

Celestine spooned rice into Andre as if he were a child in a high chair. When a grain of rice got stuck to the side of his mouth, she cleaned it off with her spoon, the way you would with a baby. Jared wondered how Celestine helped Andre in the bathroom, since Andre also couldn't use toilet paper or brush his teeth. He shuddered.

Dad glared at him.

Jared shrugged. What other reaction could a person have but a shudder?

Andre reached forward with his uneven stubs, gripped his water glass and tilted it up to drink. Only about half of it spilled.

"Well, the first thing we're doing," said Mom with the certainty that always made Jared want to live elsewhere, because when she talked like that, there was no way out, "is getting started on prosthetic hands for you, Andre. I'm calling Yale–New Haven Hospital in the morning."

This would be her new passion. Like when she started the adult day care; she'd spent a million hours getting that going. Now she was going to spend a million hours getting metal claws stuck to Andre's stumps. The only thing worse than sitting at dinner across from a guy with no hands was going to be sitting at dinner across from a guy with hooks.

Alake just sat there, in Mopsy's old fleece bathrobe with the yellow duckies appliquéd to the pockets. She must have been starving, but she didn't eat. And although Celestine fed Andre, she didn't seem to consider feeding Alake.

Mopsy got back to her questions. "Mattu, were you a child soldier?"

The rice fell off Mattu's fork. "I was *not* a child soldier. It is not a good thing to say of anybody. The child soldiers were more vicious than grown soldiers ever were."

"Why?"

"I don't know. Perhaps they did not have enough time with their mother and father or aunts and uncles or grandparents to learn about goodness. But do not ask more, I beg you. I am here to look ahead."

Shouldn't he say "we are here"? thought Jared.

"Celestine, has Alake been to school?" Mopsy asked.

"I went to mission school for six years," said Celestine, "and Andre attended for nine."

Interesting, thought Jared. She didn't answer Mopsy's question, and that wasn't what Kirk Crick said about how many years they went to school.

What's the matter with me? he asked himself. Am I actually trying to catch them out on something?

Since nobody else seemed to have noticed Alake's empty plate, Jared filled it with the same food Celestine had chosen for herself and Andre: rice and chicken. Then he picked up Alake's fork and tried to put it in her hand, but her hands remained in her lap.

Mopsy spoke with her mouth full. "Mattu, what's in your boxes, anyway?"

"The ashes of my grandparents."

Jared's mother gasped. "Your parents, Celestine? Or yours, Andre?"

There was such a long pause that everybody stopped eating. It seemed like a simple question.

"My parents," said Andre at last.

"How did they die?" demanded Mopsy.

"The rice gets cold," said Celestine. "And also the chicken."

They're not going to discuss the past, thought Jared. They don't even seem to *know* the past.

Mopsy finally noticed Alake. About time, because Jared wasn't taking her on. It was enough to have Mattu and a pair of dead grandparents in his room.

"Don't you like rice, Alake?" said Mopsy. "I can fix you something else. How about ice cream? When I'm upset, I like a big bowl of ice cream. I leave it out for a while, so it gets soft and friendly."

This was the kind of remark that made Jared want to leave for college a year early. Why did Mopsy always have to sound like a three-year-old? Why was she not struggling to become worth something? Every single marking period, her teachers would write "young for her age" on her report card, and every single time, she failed to improve.

"Mint chocolate chip?" suggested Mopsy. "Mocha swirl?"

Alake was silent.

With an insight Jared had not expected his sister to have, Mopsy said, "Why don't Alake and I eat in the other room?" She picked up Alake's plate, took her hand and led her into the little TV room off the opposite side of the kitchen. It contained a small sofa and their old television, and it was used only when people wanted to watch different shows at the same time but didn't want to go to their bedroom because then they'd be too far from the snacks.

The doorbell rang.

Celestine flung her chair back. Andre leaped to his feet, as if he planned to run somewhere. Mattu's huge eyes got huger.

"It's okay," said Jared's mom, "it's just the doorbell."

If anything, Andre and Celestine were more horrified. Like, who were they expecting? The front door opened, because Jared's parents hardly ever locked it until bedtime. "It's me," yelled the minister.

"Come on in, Pete!"

Dr. Nickerson came bounding in, looking very unministerish in his oldest tracksuit. He loved running up Prospect Hill and did it all the time; he wasn't even breathing hard. "How's everybody doing?"

Everybody—if by this, he meant the refugees—had sagged down in their chairs like stabbed balloons.

The minister held out his hand to the closest refugee, who happened to be Andre. "I'm the minister. Pete Nickerson. We're so glad to have you."

Then he saw the arm stubs.

◆

Mopsy was glad to leave the room. She couldn't stand that Andre had no hands. Mopsy had always loved God with her whole heart, just the way they told you to in Sunday school. But shouldn't God have come down from heaven and stopped Andre from having his hands chopped off? What else had he been doing that he couldn't manage that?

I mean, how busy could you be? she asked him.

Mopsy shut the door to the little TV room and pulled down the blinds in case Alake knew it was dark out. Then she eased Alake onto the old sofa. She lifted a spoonful of rice toward Alake's face. Alake took the spoon in her own hand and licked off a single grain of rice. "Excuse me," said Mopsy. "Who in the history of the world ate one rice at a time?"

Alake looked down at the plate, took it in her hand and ate like a person.

Mopsy was content. She made an executive decision and went and got Alake a can of Coke. Coca-Cola was sold worldwide, so maybe Alake would recognize the logo and feel safe with it. Mopsy yanked the pop-top and handed the fizzing can to Alake, who took a sip, swallowed, shivered and swallowed again.

Mopsy thought about taking Alake to school in the morning.

All her life, when teachers wrote reports on Mopsy, they would finish, "Young for her age." When she was eight, they said she acted five. When she was eleven, they said she acted eight. Last year she'd actually been sent to a counselor. Mopsy was humiliated. She never acted up or talked back. Didn't pick on anybody, skip homework or fail tests. What was everybody annoyed about?

Mopsy took Alake's hand in hers. Alake's fingers were

beautiful—long and elegant. The double colors of her hand fascinated Mopsy: dark and warm on top, soft and pale on the palm.

Mopsy planned how she would introduce Alake to the sixth grade, and help her talk again, and laugh, and be American.

◆

When Dr. Nickerson had recovered from the shock of finding no hands at the bottom of Andre's arms, and Andre had reassured him that it was all right, the minister fell into Mopsy's seat. Mom offered to fix him a plate. "No, thanks, Kara, I've lost my appetite."

Andre bit his lip.

"I'm sorry! I didn't mean you, Andre! I've lost my appetite because we have problems in the church that . . ." He gave up without explaining.

Jared, who never stepped into church conversations, said, "You guys want to talk in the living room? I can take care of Mr. and Mrs. Amabo."

His parents and the minister took him up on his offer and left the room. Jared hoped the church situation hadn't gotten even worse, because he was willing to help once, but he sure wasn't willing to do it twice.

"Please, Jared," said Andre. "It will be our church too. May we know what the problems are?"

"A guy everybody trusted stole all the money."

"Ah," said Andre. "Only God can be trusted."

"*You* can't trust God," said Jared irritably. "God let this nightmare happen to you to start with."

"You confuse God with man," said Andre.

Jared so didn't want to talk about God over dessert. He stuck two pies, a cake, a pan of Rice Krispies Treats and two half gallons of ice cream on the table.

"What is that?" asked Celestine, pointing to the ice cream.

"God's gift. You're gonna love it."

♦

The fifth refugee was met by a seventy-four-year-old volunteer who would drive him to the tiny apartment he was to share with two young men from Sudan. She enjoyed her refugee work, because she loved chatting, and all the Africans she had encountered spoke English. But this refugee was different. His rage was palpable. He did not want to chat. She couldn't imagine him chatting.

She almost bought him the return ticket to New York that he was demanding.

Instead, she paid his taxi fare so that she would not be alone with him.

Then she telephoned the two young men from Sudan to let them know their new roommate would be arriving momentarily.

She almost told them that she was afraid of him, but she did not want to judge.

♦

Jared was hardly ever ready for bed. He always had another hour of TV in him. But Mattu was asleep sitting up. Jared shook Mattu's shoulder and they trudged upstairs.

In the bathroom, Mattu admired his new toothbrush as excessively as Mopsy would have, which put Jared over the edge. He ran downstairs to find his parents in the kitchen, cleaning up. "What'd Dr. Nickerson have to say?" he asked.

"He wants to kill Brady. We all want to kill Brady. But it's not your typical church activity."

Jared laughed. "And how is everybody's refugee?"

"Celestine and Andre love their room," said Mom. "They especially love how the shades pull down and that there's a nightlight in the bathroom. But," she said uncertainly (Jared's mother, who was never uncertain), "they just shut the door and went to bed. They didn't check on the children." Mom was a double-checking kind of parent. Triple, sometimes.

"They checked on their kids enough to keep them alive through a civil war and get them to America," Dad pointed out. "That's pretty serious checking. And maybe these kids don't need to be tucked in. You'd grow up fast in their world. Maybe at fifteen and sixteen, they're grown-ups."

But Jared thought there was a different possibility.

Celestine and Andre were not behaving like parents.

So maybe they weren't.

Maybe Alake and Mattu were not the children of Celestine and Andre.

# CHAPTER FIVE

JARED WOKE UP STARVING TO death. He arrived in the kitchen to find all four Africans already at the breakfast table. Alake was sitting there not drinking her orange juice and not touching her Cheerios. Jared tried to see Cheerios through African eyes but failed. He waved a jelly doughnut in front of Alake's eyes.

"Jared, don't push," said his mother, as if there were any other way to get Alake going.

Mattu examined the selection of bagels, cinnamon raisin toast, blueberry and apple muffins and plain and sugar cereals. He chose one of everything and ate as if he really *were* starving to death.

Jared hadn't done any homework, because going to the airport had taken the whole day, not to mention the time he'd lost due to the shock of getting refugees to start with. The high school would totally accept refugees as an excuse for staying home, and he was planning on a long, happy breakfast and a little TV.

Mopsy was the kind of person who couldn't bear to miss school. She still loved her teachers, something Jared had outgrown in second grade. Maybe first. Now that he thought about it, he hadn't been all that fond of his kindergarten teacher.

Mopsy said, "Alake goes to school with me today."

"But what can she do in school?" asked Mattu. "She just sits. Will the teacher not be angry?"

"No, they'll try to make her comfortable," said Mom, as if Alake were dying in hospice, "and then do some testing."

Jared wanted to know how testing was going to work on a person who was mute and blind, but he let it go.

"And since Alake is happy with Mopsy . . . ," Mom began.

Alake doesn't do "happy" any more than she does "unhappy," Jared thought. Alake is just there.

". . . and since hanging around the house would be boring for poor Alake . . ."

Jared rolled his eyes. What does Alake know about boring? It's all boring if you're unconscious.

Mopsy, predictably, clapped her hands and danced in a circle around Alake, who did not notice. Alake was wearing yesterday's yellow pants and faded cotton T-shirt, washed and pressed by Mom. "She needs something better to wear," said Mopsy. "This isn't pretty and it has no style."

"Raid my closet," said Mom. "She's my height."

"Your stuff is middle-aged, Mom. First days of school are very important, even if you're from Africa. Maybe especially if you're from Africa. She has to look good."

"She looks better than good," Mom pointed out. "She's beautiful."

This was where most American parents would chime in. Always compliment: that was the American rule. But Andre and Celestine remained silent.

"Are we also going to school?" Mattu asked Jared. And then in a whisper, as if praying, he breathed, "I would love to go to school."

Fine, they'd go to school. Grumpily, Jared picked out decent clothes for Mattu. Jared liked his clothing baggy, so it was not that hard to fit a person several inches taller. He wanted Mattu wearing exactly what everybody else wore. Jared was actually a little worried about the reception an African might get in a school nearly all white. He could think of quite a few guys who were always trolling around for somebody to pick on. The British accent helped, but the right clothes would stack the deck in Mattu's favor.

Mopsy replaced Alake's shabby outfit with a sleek lime green sweater and crisp black pants. Since Alake was starvation thin, the clothes hung as if Alake weren't even in them. Mom kissed Alake good-bye, which Alake noticed no more than she would the wind, but when Mom kissed Mattu's cheek, he stepped back and gaped at her.

Mom giggled. "Have a lovely first day of school," she said, because she was the kind of person who actually believed that first days of school could be lovely. "I'll be taking your parents shopping for clothes and shoes and handbags." Mom cared deeply about handbags, which she changed to match every outfit, but her real love was shoes. She had an entire closet for shoes.

Mattu put his hand to his cheek where Jared's mom had kissed him. Jared thought he was kind of happy about it. But maybe not. Jared went outside. Mattu stepped out with him and immediately froze like a cartoon, eyes flickering left and right, peering through the trees. Jared almost said, What? You think man-eating lions are hanging out in the hemlocks? But he restrained himself and looked back to see how Mopsy was doing. She was going to have a seriously weird day, presenting a girl from Africa who didn't speak and wasn't going to lift a pencil.

Mopsy was literally pulling Alake out the door. Good thing Jared didn't have to take Alake. If he showed up shoving some girl into school, they'd probably arrest him.

Celestine and Andre did not say good-bye, wish their kids luck or give them a hug. So Jared's guess was right, and these were not Mattu and Alake's parents...or they were the parents and didn't like their kids...or African families were really different from American families.

It was still early in the morning and very chilly, but the slanted rays of the sun were strong. When Alake turned her head from the bright light, her eyes narrowed. She looked hard and scary and used up. She had no shape under the clothing, and no stranger could have said whether she was a girl or boy, whether she was ten years old or twenty.

*These people could be anybody.*

Cell phones were not allowed in either the high school or the middle school. Jared always took his anyway, to use in the hall or at lunch or under the desk, but Mopsy, naturally, obeyed and never took her phone. Jared ran back in, scooped her cell off its charger in the kitchen and caught up to his sister. "Keep your phone on. If you need me, call. If the teachers whine about it, tell them you have to stay in touch because of Alake."

Mopsy was delighted. She took the phone proudly, as if it symbolized something, and tucked it in the outside phone pocket of her book bag.

Alake's eyes drifted toward the phone.

◆

In Austin, the two young men from Sudan lay awake all night. They did not talk to each other. There was no need.

Eventually the fifth refugee fell into that deep, almost comatose sleep of one who has traveled many hours and crossed several time zones.

At dawn the other two slipped out, abandoning the apartment to Victor. When they were safely away, they used Luke's cell phone—it was common for Christian Africans to have biblical names—and left a message at the refugee agency. "This is the kind of man we left behind. We will find somewhere else to live. Do not tell this man where we go. Do not give him our phone number. Do not tell him where we work."

◆

Mopsy stood Alake like a totem pole in front of the sixth-grade class. "This," she announced, "is Alake. Isn't that a pretty name? Alake is one of the refugees I've been telling you that our church is sponsoring, but what we didn't expect is, they're living at my house. Alake's my roommate. But there's a problem we didn't know about. Alake has had a terrible shock from all the war and killing and she stopped speaking. So we'll talk to her, but she won't talk to us. Come on, Alake, sit by me."

Mopsy had presented Alake's case so easily that even the teachers accepted her explanation. Class took place around Alake, but nobody tried to make her part of it. Alake not only didn't talk, she didn't look at the other sixth graders, didn't look out at the schoolyard and didn't look down at the book Mopsy was trying to share.

"She's not exactly like a person, is she?" whispered Quinnie. "She's more like a doll you prop up in a chair."

"Shhh, Quinnie. She speaks English."

"How do you know?"

Mopsy frowned. How *did* she know? "Well, the others speak English," she said defensively, and got a queer little shiver in her spine. She had not said "Alake's mom and dad and brother speak English." She had said "the others."

Because the four Africans did not give off the aura of family.

In fact, Mopsy didn't know how Alake's name was pronounced because none of the other three had spoken it. Names were so important. Was Alake Amabo nameless inside her own family?

Third period, a counselor came to take Alake for testing, but Alake did not move, so Mopsy went first, pulling Alake by the hand.

"Like a mutt learning how to heel," said one of the boys, and several kids laughed.

Mopsy had not known that her classmates would be mean. What was she going to do about the boy and the laughter? She hoped Alake had not understood.

In the counselor's office, Alake did not pick up the pencil to mark answers, nor did she even seem to hear the questions. The counselor couldn't do simple visual tests because Alake never saw the computer screen.

"This is beyond me," said the counselor. "I guess first we should have her hearing tested. When does she go to the doctor?"

The principal and the nurse joined them. "You can't just bring her to school, Mopsy," said the principal angrily. "We have to have papers proving that Alake has had her shots."

Mopsy produced the papers provided by the Refugee Aid Society.

The nurse was not impressed. "These are photocopies. They're not dated, and they don't even have her name. They're just stuff. Go to your regular doctor and have her get all her shots."

"But she might end up getting an extra one," protested Mopsy, who could think of nothing worse than an unnecessary needle. Then she remembered Andre's arms.

The nurse shrugged.

Mopsy stood her ground. "Alake is a refugee. The definition of a refugee is, they didn't have time to grab their paperwork. They were running. They barely escaped with their lives."

"That's what they claim," said the nurse with a sniff. "Some people will tell any old lie to come to America."

Mopsy, who loved everybody, now hated several boys in class plus the nurse. "Alake, don't listen to her. I know you didn't tell any lies."

Alake's eyelids quivered, which Mopsy figured was a sign of strong emotion.

In the cafeteria line, Alake would not pick up a tray or touch the food, so Mopsy loaded a tray with stuff normal people liked and went to her favorite table, where everybody made room and said hello and then took offense because Alake wasn't grateful to be welcomed. "Get over it!" snapped Mopsy. "Alake is doing the best she can."

Mopsy never snapped at anybody, so her friends giggled and got over it.

Mopsy set a little place for Alake, with plate, fork, spoon and drink. She named the foods and chatted about how yummy every-thing was. Mopsy's friends couldn't say whatever they were think-ing, so the topic of Africans living in your bedroom was not mentioned and instead they discussed television. Everybody had watched different shows the night before, so they filled each other in.

Mopsy was pretty sure that Alake's eyes had now fastened on her food. But they were going to run out of lunchtime before

Alake made the decision to chew or not to chew. Since everybody else liked five minutes in the bathroom to gossip and fix their hair, and two or three minutes to saunter back to class, the other girls left while Mopsy and Alake continued to sit.

Alake watched them go.

Mopsy was pleased. Alake knew that things were happening and one day she would jump in.

I will totally save her, thought Mopsy proudly.

♦

Mattu's first period was spent in Guidance, with the principal, two counselors and the school nurse hanging over him. Nobody was happy with the paperwork Mattu was presenting. Jared was glad somebody was sitting up and taking notice that this was seriously skimpy paperwork to change countries by. But he said, "A person getting murdered doesn't stop to grab a list of the dates when he got shots." He wanted to point out Mattu's scar, so that they would realize how fast Mattu had had to run. But Mattu was sitting so that the adults didn't see that side of his face, and Jared didn't want to treat him like an art exhibit or something—See this line? Its meaning is fear and speed.

"Tell us about the school you attended, Mattu," said the principal.

Mattu spread his hands in a sort of shrug. They looked like basketball hands. Jared passionately loved basketball and was not good at it. He had a painful vision of Mattu being really good at everything.

"I finished fourth grade," said Mattu. "Then, for several years of war, nothing. Then, in the refugee camp, missionary teachers."

"We've got to do lots of testing, then," said the counselor, thrilled at the prospect of making somebody suffer through all that.

"I promised Mattu he could hang out in class with me for the first day or two," said Jared.

The argument was won by Mattu's pleading eyes, way bigger than American eyes, with a way bigger effect on the principal.

They arrived late for American history, but Mrs. Dowling beamed. "Mattu, we are so glad to have you. Your presence will make class much more interesting, with new viewpoints and experiences."

In his beautiful English, Mattu said, "I thank you for your welcome. I am in your class with joy and respect."

Wow. Well, he was the only one. Mrs. Dowling was not popular.

Most of the kids giggled, but Tay, who was a pistol and could start anybody off in any direction, smiled at Mattu. "My father would love you, Mattu. He's been waiting all his life for me to say things like that. And your English is excellent. Better than ours."

Tay was one of those people who did not need a last name; nobody else in the town, maybe the state, was named Tay. She had gone through eighth grade at the Country Day School and convinced her parents to let her attend public high school. They weren't happy about her choice, and they really weren't happy about the academic standards (none, they said). From her golf game to her tan, from her yellow hair to her Latin verbs, Tay was above and beyond any other girl at school, and way out of Jared's league.

Jared got an extra chair, pulled it next to his desk, gestured Mattu into it and opened his history book, confident that it was not going to matter whether he'd read the chapter.

"English is my native tongue," Mattu explained to Tay. He sat down, running his hands along the desk and excitedly stroking the textbook. He did not seem bothered at being the only black kid; rather, he behaved as if he were the norm and the white kids were a diorama at the natural history museum.

"You must have an African tongue," insisted Tay.

"We speak a tribal language at home," agreed Mattu politely.

It occurred to Jared that he had not heard any Amabo speak to any other Amabo.

"But mostly we speak English," said Mattu, "because Sierra Leone was once an English colony."

You're from Liberia, thought Jared. Kirk Crick said so. Liberia was never an English colony. It was founded by freed American slaves who went back to Africa.

"I got it wrong, then," said Mrs. Dowling. "I thought when she telephoned this morning that Jared's mother said you were from Liberia."

Mattu paused.

To think? wondered Jared. Or to think up lies?

"Because of civil wars, we had to flee from Sierra Leone to Liberia, where we lived until the war shifted and we crossed the border again. Then war broke out in the very place we hoped to be safe, and after many sorrows and much danger, we arrived in Nigeria. There was much confusion. If I may, I prefer not to discuss it."

Tay discussed whatever she felt like discussing. "I thought a person from a refugee camp would be half starved. You look pretty good to me, Mattu."

She was flirting, but Mattu didn't realize it. Very seriously he explained, "Food, mainly rice, is distributed. At times there is more food in the refugee camp than people in the host country have. There are riots if the refugees can eat and the native people cannot."

"I'd just love you to give us a talk about Sierra Leone culture and the Mende tribe," said Mrs. Dowling.

Mattu's face was blank.

He doesn't know anything about Sierra Leone or its culture, thought Jared. Maybe he's not from *either* of those countries! Maybe he and Celestine and Andre and Alake don't even come from the same country. They can't talk about their background because they don't share one. They can't talk in their tribal tongue because it isn't the same one. They can't talk about their escape because they didn't do it together. This is just a set of people. They needed to get out and they used each other. And now they're using my family.

Next time that refugee officer showed up, Jared was telling.

These people shouldn't get away with what they'd done, any more than Brady Wall should get away with what he'd done.

Jared wondered how Mopsy was faring with Alake. God help Mopsy.

◆

Alake almost knew where she was.

She almost knew that she was attending school.

The memory that plagued her life—if this was living—was a school memory.

Alake had been wearing her school uniform. She loved how clean and special it was, with its two deep front pockets. Alake loved pockets, and the way you could slip your treasures into them.

Everybody in Alake's compound had moved outside into the blazing hot sun. She did not know why this had happened. Had they been going somewhere? Had they thought there was time to run? Or were they just waving good-bye as the girls left for school?

It turned out not to matter.

Victor's people mowed every one of them down with machine guns.

Only Alake and her sister were left standing. Alake didn't know why, and probably Victor didn't know either. He didn't have a purpose for anything. He did things because he could.

Alake had her hands tucked in her pockets. Maybe that was why Victor grabbed Alake's sister instead—her hand was out.

Perhaps Victor had meant to take Alake's sister into the worst future on earth—to be a child soldier. Perhaps he had planned to rape her before killing her. But Alake's sister wrenched free and fled to Alake, screaming, "Don't let him hurt me!"

Alake took her hands out of her pockets and wrapped her arms around her sister, thinking, They will kill us now. There's no time to be afraid. At least I will be holding her when it happens.

But Victor—of course, she had not known his name then; she learned it later—did not order his boy soldiers to kill Alake and her sister. He ordered them to surround the school. In her memory, the school was next to her house, even though she knew the school was quite a walk upriver.

How had they gotten to the school, Alake and her sister?

Why hadn't Alake and her sister taken advantage when the soldiers' attention was elsewhere? Why hadn't they run into the bush?

The school was not a building in the sense that this American school was. It had a roof for shade. It had benches. There was a shelf of books. Alake used to love when it was her turn to hold a book and read. The school did not have walls to speak of, so when the machine guns fired, the children on the benches, the children on the floor and the children already running were cut down.

The barrage of fire missed the two teachers.

When the echoes died down and the blood ceased to spatter, Alake stood there holding her sister, and the teachers stood there staring at their fate.

Perhaps Victor was a man easily bored by the same old killing. Perhaps that was why he hurled Alake's sister across the packed

dirt to land halfway between the monstrous laughing child soldiers and the terrified silent teachers.

"You want your sister to live?" asked Victor.

Of course Alake wanted her sister to live.

Victor handed the machine gun to Alake. "Kill your teachers
and I will let your sister go."

♦

Since Jared never prayed, "God help Mopsy" had no meaning.
If there *was* a God and Jared prayed, God might take it too seriously
and expect Jared to get into the habit or something. If there *wasn't*
a God, Jared didn't want to be a jerk, praying to nothing.

But Jared didn't like how Alake's eyes had moved that morning. Toward the phone. These people who supposedly had never
used one and had had their first telephone experience in the van.
If Jared's guesses were right, Alake could have grown up using a
phone. Maybe her eyes flickered over that phone because she
knew somebody to call. Maybe she could talk just fine.

God, thought Jared, stressing the words differently, help
Mopsy.

A little shiver ran down the back of his eyes, as if the prayer
had lodged there, cold and true.

No, *I* am cold, thought Jared. Who am I to turn these guys in?
And there's no comparison to Brady Wall. These guys didn't steal
anything. They just fibbed a little. I'd tell a lie or two—or several
hundred—to get out of a refugee camp.

Jared almost thanked God for this insight, but he got a grip. "Let's cut Mattu a little slack," he said to Tay, "and just have class instead of grilling him."

"Okay, fine," said Tay, blowing Jared a kiss.

Jared came dangerously close to catching the invisible kiss and keeping it. I am not Mopsy, he reminded himself. I will never ever behave like Mopsy. Death would be better.

School went by at a dizzying pace, which never happened to Jared. Normally, school crawled. Suddenly they were in the last class of the day, phys ed. "Stands for 'physical education,'" explained Jared. "Sports and games, which we usually call gym, short for 'gymnasium.'"

Mattu had never seen a gymnasium. The shining yellow wood floors with their brightly painted lines, the bleachers, basketball nets, pennants commemorating victories, locker rooms—all required explanation. Mattu touched every surface, especially the shiny ones. "In Africa, there would be dust. The wind always blows; the dust always spreads. Unless it's rainy season. Then—mud."

Outside the boys' locker room were three pay phones, installed in the olden days, when nobody had a cell phone. Jared had never used a pay phone.

Mattu's eyes landed on the phones.

"Phone calls are cheaper and easier from home," Jared told him.

"I don't know anyone to call. I am just amazed at how telephones are everywhere. In every pocket, in every hall."

"Jared Finch!" shouted the coach. "Get a move on!"

Jared and Mattu yanked on gym shorts, and since Mattu said he loved soccer, and since Africans were supposed to be seriously good at soccer, Coach took them outside, saying that it was very warm today, forty-three degrees, stop whimpering. It was probably worth the sacrifice, because Mattu was seriously good.

"Go, Mattu!" shouted the boys. "You're a gladiator!"

Six minutes later the coach had to take Mattu out. "It's a game, see," he said. He was laughing, because with Mattu on board, they could whip the league. "You're still at war, Mattu. But in the suburbs we sort of frown on killing people over a soccer goal."

Mattu nodded seriously, as if he might write this American philosophy down.

Standing on the sidelines was Daniel, one of the few black kids in school. His mother was a professor at the University of Connecticut and drove all the way to Storrs every day, while his father was a dermatologist and drove all the way to New Haven. Basically Daniel never saw his parents, who were lucky that Daniel wasn't a troublemaker. Jared had thought of calling Daniel up the day before: Hey. We're taking in a black family. Thought you'd like to know. You could be special friends.

He had decided against it.

Daniel wasn't taking gym today: he managed to sit out often and Jared never knew why. Or cared. Daniel walked over to Jared. "You didn't tell me."

"I didn't know. They were supposed to live somewhere else, but the apartment fell through, so my parents volunteered."

"What's he like?"

"Hard to say. Mainly he's polite. You want to meet him?"

Daniel considered this.

He's worried that Mattu will become his burden, thought Jared. That their skin color will chain them together.

The word "chain" seemed an unfortunate choice, since Daniel's ancestors had to have been slaves, and Jared tried to delete it from his thoughts, but it sat there. It occurred to him that if the four Amabos were not joined by blood, they were now chained to each other by paperwork.

Mattu was visibly joyful to see another black person. He trotted over, hand extended to shake Daniel's, a smile as huge as his eyes illuminating his face. When they had introduced themselves, Mattu said, "You do not play soccer, Daniel?"

"I hate sports."

Jared laughed. "How do you get out of gym so often, anyway? I didn't think hating it was an excuse."

"I fake illnesses. Today I'm faking a chest cold."

"Which would stop you how, exactly, from playing soccer?" Jared demanded.

"I'm so bad at every sport, the gym teachers are thrilled to have me on the sidelines."

"We laugh at what?" asked Mattu.

"Me," said Daniel, smiling. "My parents are way into eating out, Mattu. You guys like fish? There's a terrific fish house down the road."

Mattu had no idea what Daniel was saying.

"He's inviting the four of you for dinner at a restaurant," said Jared.

Mattu got flustered. Jared could think of plenty of reasons: Andre's lack of arms, Alake's lack of speech, the general lack of family togetherness, failure to know what country they were from...

"Or maybe we should wait a while," said Daniel. "Till everybody's settled in."

Mattu was obviously relieved.

Jared was not. What did "settled in" mean? Weren't "settlers" people who never left?

♦

Neither Andre nor Celestine asked the children how their first day at school had been. Jared's mom did not notice. "Everybody in the car!" she called. "We're headed for Super Stop and Shop."

"Not me," said Jared. "I have homework."

"No," said his mother. "We need a ratio of one of us to one of them, and we're already short because Dad isn't home from work yet."

Jared hated grocery shopping. It was enough that he'd taken Mattu to school.

"No, you can't get out of it," said his mother. "You do any whining, Jared, and you can go live with Aunt Valerie."

This was a huge threat. Aunt Valerie had given up her job as a stockbroker and bought a run-down farm in northwest New

York, where the lake effect dumped a thousand feet of snow every year. She was now raising llamas. Visiting Aunt Valerie consisted of shoveling manure in bad weather.

Jared had to laugh.

At the huge Stop & Shop, Celestine and Andre were enchanted by the metal-fence-like things on wheels called carts. They shared one, and then Mattu wanted one too, and then didn't Mopsy yank a cart out for Alake? Alake did not look at Mopsy, let alone put her fingers on the handle. This didn't bother Mopsy, who loved grocery shopping. She bounced up and down the aisles like some horrifying toy whose batteries you prayed would run down, but they never did. So here was Jared in an actual parade of carts.

They entered vegetable territory. Jared had only the mildest interest in green food, so he hardly glanced. But the Amabo family stopped short. Celestine gave a little cry. Mattu whispered to Jared, "Is all that real?"

"We need two kinds of potatoes," said Mom. "Boiling for mashed and Idaho for baking. We want lettuce, cucumbers, tomatoes, celery and radishes for salad, and of course fruit—let's see what looks good."

Her guests were spellbound by the stacks and piles, bins and bags of gleaming, clean, misted, perfect food.

Mattu, who had touched every surface in the gym, now needed to touch every vegetable. Andre sang out the names of everything he recognized and demanded words for everything he did not, so he and Mom became a little chorus.

Andre: "What is that?"

Mom: "Cauliflower."

Andre: "Oh! Cauliflower!"

Jared died several deaths, but nobody was watching; they were too busy with their own lists and whiny kids, and for all Jared knew, they were just as excited by cauliflower.

His mother tossed food into her cart with the practiced hand of many years' shopping. Celestine whispered, "Hot peppers, perhaps?"

Mom's idea of spice was salt, so she had never bought a hot pepper. But there they were, separate from the fat salad-type peppers. "You pick," she told Celestine.

Celestine couldn't quite bring herself to touch them. "I have no money. This will cost a great deal."

"The church raised money for groceries. I've got cash in my purse that is actually yours, and when we get to checkout, you'll actually pay for it." Mom took out a white envelope and opened the flap to show Celestine a thick wad of bills.

But Celestine was studying the people in matching store jackets.

"They work here," explained Jared.

"Oh, my! Could I work here too?" Celestine asked Mom, hardly daring to hope.

"I've gotten you a job at a motel, but we can come back another time and interview here. Keep moving, we don't have all day. Bread!" Mom yelled, as if she were in charge of bingo. Mopsy, who had high bread standards, tried to get there first so she could give bread orders. Mattu could hardly wait to see bread and was speeding around the corner. Jared hoped he wouldn't take down a tower of canned goods. Jared would have to go wait in the car if anything that humiliating happened.

Alake was left standing in the fruit aisle. Nobody in her family had noticed her. Even Mopsy had forgotten her.

Long, thin brown fingers shivering, Alake reached toward a tower of polished red apples. Her fingers closed on the top apple. She slid it under her shirt.

"We can get all the food you want, Alake," said Jared. "But we have to buy it." He gently tugged her wrist until the apple appeared again. "It's not a good thing in America to take the apple without paying."

Alake nodded.

She knows what I said, he thought.

Alake held the apple out in front of her.

"I'll teach you American money when we get to checkout, okay?" said Jared.

They were in the store almost another hour, and she never let the precious apple sag.

# CHAPTER SIX

THEY WERE LATE FOR CHURCH, not because the Amabos weren't ready, but because Dad wasn't. "Instead of going to our church," he said, "let's go to our sister church in New Haven. Most of that congregation is black. They'd be so excited to meet you and share in welcoming you, and you're probably sick of nobody but white people around."

Celestine and Andre were even more amazed by this suggestion than Jared. "No, thank you," said Celestine. "We will go to the church which is sponsoring us and paying for our groceries. It is our church now."

"You're just looking for an excuse to be somewhere else, Dad," said Mopsy.

"It is a terrible sorrow," agreed Celestine, "that a man you trusted stole from you. Trust broken is worse than money taken."

Jared hadn't known until his little sister said so that their father was so upset he didn't want to show up at his own church. And Jared hadn't known until an African refugee said so that it wasn't about the money.

Celestine wore her glorious headpiece and her ferociously

colored wrap, while Mopsy had put Alake into a hot pink pants suit of Mom's that Mom never wore because it was gaudy. As long as you didn't notice her hair, Alake looked as if she had just fallen off a runway at some important fashion show. It was impossible, however, not to notice her hair.

Mattu insisted on wearing a suit of Dad's. The pant legs showed several inches of ankle and the sleeves exposed several inches of wrist. This was meaningless to Mattu.

Andre chose a sports jacket from the clothing donation pile and did not mind that no hands showed at the bottom of the cuffs.

They sat in the front row at church. Latecomers always had to sit in front, because the back pews filled first. People liked to survey their friends and neighbors, but they didn't want to *be* surveyed. Jared hated sitting in front.

It was a good hymn day, though, with all three hymns worth singing. This was not always the case. Sometimes singing was the low point of the hour. They opened with "We gather together to ask the Lord's blessing," usually a Thanksgiving hymn. Because, Dr. Nickerson explained, we are giving thanks for the presence of the Amabo family.

Andre had a fine, rich tenor. People took notice. Who is this guy? Let's get him in the choir. How amazing that Andre would know hymns at all, let alone this one, and that he could so easily read the difficult, old-fashioned verses.

Everywhere I turn, I'm a racist, thought Jared. I thought they'd be just a little bit literate.

Jared listened to the sermon, which he rarely did. He was generally lost in thoughts of the car he would one day own or songs he planned to download.

The minister had latched on to the word "inn" in the story of the Good Samaritan, where the good guy rescues a hurt stranger and carries him to an inn. The good guy has places to go and people to see, so he pays the innkeeper to take care of the hurt guy and moves on. It was a good text for discussing refugees. We the church are paying the bills, explained Dr. Nickerson, while the Finches are providing the inn.

Bet the innkeeper didn't have to share his bedroom, thought Jared. Bet the innkeeper lived in a separate wing.

Dr. Nickerson made no mention of Brady Wall's theft. Instead, he had a letter to the congregation printed in the bulletin. Jared never read stuff that wasn't required, making him the only person in church actually listening to the sermon, because everybody else was reading up on their new financial and legal nightmare. The minister ended on a warm, welcoming note, asking Celestine, Andre, Mattu and Alake to stand and make themselves known—like there could be any doubt which ones were from Africa.

Afterward there was a special coffee hour and a receiving line. Since a crucial member of the receiving line didn't shake hands, and since the supposedly competent adults were off discussing Brady Wall, Jared stepped between Andre and the first eager hand shaker. "Africans bow," he said, and demonstrated. Andre gave Jared a particularly sweet smile and bowed to a family of Americans, who giggled as one and bowed back.

♦

The restaurant Mom had chosen for Sunday dinner had deep, dark booths. Jared always preferred a booth, but especially today, because then nobody would see Celestine feeding Andre.

"That was a fine service," said Celestine. "Each week I will look forward to hearing the word of God."

"God is good," agreed Andre.

Jared could not let this pass. "Andre, somebody chopped off your hands. That's evil. And you run around saying God is good? If God was good, he wouldn't have let that happen."

"It was not the fault of God," said Andre.

"Well, he should have stepped in and stopped it," said Jared.

Andre grinned. "I would have been glad to see Him."

Mopsy leaned forward. "Andre, have you ever met anybody who actually saw God?"

"In our hearts, we have all seen God. God kept me going when there was nothing else."

"You would have kept going anyway, because of your children," said Mopsy with American certainty.

Andre looked puzzled.

Because he doesn't have children, Jared thought.

Mattu tilted his large menu. "An entire page lists only things to drink."

One thing these guys did well—change the subject. "Right," said Jared. "Ten ways to have coffee, three kinds of Coke—"

"I can read," said Mattu irritably.

Mopsy giggled. "Isn't Jared annoying? How are you doing sharing a room? Does it make the refugee camp look good?"

Mattu smiled at Mopsy. "Nothing would make a refugee camp look good. And I love this list of things to drink. Once when I was on the run, I was so thirsty, I knelt down and drank the urine of a cow puddled in its hoofprint."

Andre nodded. "When I was that thirsty, I used to put rocks in my mouth. Somehow it felt damp to the tongue."

"You were that bad off," demanded Jared, "and still you think God is good? You've been praying to him all this time, he should do a little something for you."

"He brought me here," Andre pointed out.

"Which reminds me," said Mom brightly. "The newspaper called. They want your thoughts about America."

So that was why Mom had been vacuuming and plumping pillows.

"No," said Celestine.

Mom's cheeks were very pink. "The media tends not to cover Africa. I have collected statistics. Congo had about a million displaced persons during their civil war. Two million each had to flee Sierra Leone, Somalia and Liberia. And there's Sudan. Angola. Rwanda. Americans would be more touched by your story than by statistics. Africa needs the publicity. If we personalize the civil war—"

"Mom," said Mopsy sharply. "Andre does not want to be photographed. Celestine does not want to be a story. That's that."

This actually shut their mother up. Jared was impressed.

The waitress brought their meals.

"I'm the hamburger," called Mopsy. "It's not too well done or too rare, is it? It has to be perfect or I can't eat it." Mopsy cut into her hamburger to check its perfection level.

The Africans watched in silent astonishment. Probably in Africa, if you had anything to eat, it was perfect.

Dad was just sitting there. He wasn't part of the conversation. He didn't even seem like part of the family. It was Andre who said softly. "Let us thank our Lord Jesus Christ for the many blessings which surround us."

Since they were nicely hidden, Jared didn't mind holding hands. He reached out automatically to form the circle and then yanked his fingers away just before they touched the hideous stub above Andre's wrist. He set his hand on Andre's shoulder instead.

A shoulder was what you used when you shrugged. Andre still possessed shoulders. He could shrug. But he didn't. He thanked the Lord for the many blessings that surrounded him.

◆

Of thirty-nine days, five were already gone.

Victor did not know where New York City was or how to get

there. He did know, from having looked out the window on that plane, that he would have to cross a vast amount of land.

The refugee officer said that while of *course* Victor could live anywhere, he had to have a *job* there, and *housing*, and once he had his Social Security number, he would need to work *hard*, *very* hard, and save money, and get to New York on his *own*.

The cash Victor was given hardly bought one meal. Victor solved this problem. There were plenty of elderly and crippled to prey on.

♦

Death was fascinating, but Mopsy had no firsthand knowledge of it.

Death showed up on television a lot. If you watched police or lawyer shows or soap operas, people were always dying—murder, car accident, suicide or the result of stupidity or some crazy stunt. And of course, if you watched the news, the most important thing after sports and weather was always the number of people killed in battle or dying in some plague (probably in another country) or committing crimes in some grim city (probably just down the road). Mopsy also loved a paperback series in which yet another beautiful girl got a dread disease but faced death bravely, surrounded by friends.

Now death was right in Mopsy's house.

Two unburied people sitting on a shelf.

It was not wise to go into Jared's personal space, because (talk about death) Jared would kill her.

Mopsy waited. The afternoon came, when Jared was out in the driveway with Andre, and Alake and Mattu were snacking in the kitchen with Mom. Or at least, Mattu was snacking. Alake was probably just sitting in front of her snack.

Mopsy ran upstairs and slipped into her brother's room.

Mopsy could hardly get lunch money to school without losing it. How remarkable that Mattu had carried his grandparents' ashes around the world with barely a dent or a crease in the boxes. Of course, Mattu was very cute and a refugee and all, so the flight attendants had probably bent the rules for him, especially when he spoke with his adorable English accent, and let him hold the boxes in his lap the whole way.

Mopsy slid one finger under a flap. It lifted easily. She peeked. There were flakes like charcoal ash but also grit like cat litter, and many bits the size of peas and marbles. Imagine cooking your grandparents. Mopsy gave the box a shake to make the ash settle more, so she could see farther down.

Something glowed.

Mopsy almost dropped the box.

She gave herself a moment's rest and then shook the box again and peeked. Now two bits of bone glowed.

Haunted ashes.

Mopsy closed the box and turned to flee. It's got my finger-prints on it now, she thought. It would be just like Jared to check and to find out if I touched—

In the doorway stood Alake.

Alake did not appear to have seen anything or thought about anything. She was just there.

Mopsy had the ghastly thought that Alake herself was nothing but ashes, her heart beating but her soul charred and dead.

♦

Mattu seemed fine riding home next to Jared on the bus, but each day, when he left its shelter, he seemed desperate to get back inside someplace. Again today Mattu raced up Prospect Hill while Jared trudged slowly behind him. What was there for Mattu to be afraid of outside that didn't exist inside? By now Mattu had to know that there weren't enemy soldiers or wild animals around, preparing to ambush him. The only thing that should actually frighten the Africans was getting deported—and why would that be more likely outdoors?

Mattu darted in the side door as Andre hurried out to greet Jared.

That was your son speeding by, thought Jared. You might say hi now and then.

"There's a bike hanging on the wall in the garage," said Andre excitedly.

"You want to ride it? I'll get it down for you." Jared headed into the garage, where the bike hung on big yellow hooks, but Andre beat him to it, lifting the bike easily, using his stumps. The bike had foot brakes and no gears, so it could be ridden without hands, a skill Jared had never mastered.

Andre rode back and forth on the long, flat driveway. You couldn't tell he was handless; it just looked as if he'd folded his arms over his chest. He used the longer stub to turn the handle.

"I'll walk the bike downhill for you and you can ride around town, where it's flat," suggested Jared.

Andre stared down the hill. He swallowed. "Thank you. I will go by myself."

He's older than my father, thought Jared. And scared of going alone. And brave enough to try. And who am I, who have never known fear, to say there's nothing to be afraid of? "Take my cell phone, Andre. If you need me, you can call." He was handing it to Andre when he realized there was a reason for the English expression "handing." It took hands. "I guess you'd have to go into a store or something," said Jared lamely, "and ask them to call for you."

"I will be fine." Andre pushed off, managed the first curve and was out of sight.

◆

Alake knew well what was inside the boxes. A shadow of death. Alake knew all there was to know about death. Because on that day when Victor had thrust his machine gun at her, Alake had not taken it.

It fell to the ground. The impact made it shoot by itself. The weapon did a horrifying little dance as it emptied. The child soldiers giggled when one of the soldiers was hit and blood spurted.

Victor picked up the gun. He wrapped Alake's fingers around it so she was holding it the right way. His thick yellow fingernails cut into her flesh. "You want your sister to live?"

Of course she wanted her sister to live.

Victor closed his hand over hers and aimed the machine gun at the teachers. "Pull on this."

◆

Just preparing dinner was an event.

Celestine had never used an indoor stove. Had never heard of a microwave.

Mom had to teach Celestine that the black glass cooktop would get hot just from twisting a little knob, that the pan had to be centered on this thing called a burner, that a Teflon pan could be touched only by a rubber spoon.

Mattu could not get the concept that he could slice onions and celery only on the cutting board and not on the granite counter. "Then what is this surface for?" he asked.

"It's just for resting things on," explained Jared, and even to Jared, this sounded pretty stupid.

Alake did nothing.

"Alake, help set the table," said Mopsy, who loved setting the table, another example of her maddening tendencies. What kind of person loved setting a table? A three-year-old person, maybe. But here was Mopsy, excitedly folding napkins. "Do what I do, Alake," she cried. "See how the forks go on the left?"

"Peel the potatoes," Mom ordered Jared.

"Mom, if you have to do that much work to get food, skip it and boil noodles instead."

"It's a teaching moment," said his mother. "Show Mattu how."

Two potatoes later and Jared just wanted to show the Amabo family how to move out.

◆

Time was slipping away.

Thirty-one days were left.

Victor was driven to his first day of work. Although his paperwork stated he had computer expertise, Victor had never seen a computer. The company wanted to be generous and found him a job in maintenance instead.

Victor had not come to America to vacuum carpets.

◆

The first day of having Alake at school had been fun for Mopsy. But Alake did not improve. Mopsy's friends drifted away. At home, she got no help from her mom or dad. The Finches had turned into a weird, complex family of eight, with Dad always at work or a meeting about Brady Wall and Mom being Teacher of the Year for Celestine and Andre.

The medical committee was working on fake hands for

Andre. Mopsy hoped the Amabos would be in their own apartment before Andre got hooks. Then Andre showed her a photograph. His future hand looked more like a plastic glove for doing dishes, one less worry for Mopsy.

Celestine started her job cleaning bathrooms at the motel. Mom worried because Celestine didn't know the difference between toilet cleansers and champagne. But the manager shrugged. "Our training program allows for that. She'll be fine."

On her first day, Celestine learned to fold the end of the toilet paper roll into a V. Jared and Mopsy laughed hysterically. "Normal people don't fold, Celestine," said Mopsy. "You have just acquired an utterly useless skill."

"That's what the girls told me."

"What girls?"

"The ones I work with," said Celestine. "They speak little English; instead, mostly Spanish, which I can't understand. But Bob says in one month, I might very well be the one in charge, because I can talk to the guests. I have to work on my accent. Tonight when we watch TV, I will repeat out loud everything they say."

Mopsy giggled. "Better pick a nice channel."

The doorbell rang. The Amabos fell apart again, and even though it was just Kirk Crick, they did not calm down. They had no problems, they assured him. Everything was perfect, the Finches were the best family on earth. "You never need to come again," said Celestine firmly.

"No complaint brought me here," said Kirk Crick. "I'm just saying hi. And even if you don't need me, Kara or Drew might."

Andre and Celestine vanished into their bedroom. Mattu fled upstairs, claiming to have homework. Even Alake disappeared.

Mopsy didn't think Mom or Dad needed Kirk Crick, but certainly Alake did. But Before Mopsy could list Alake's problems, her mother said, "Celestine's job is not fulfilling. There's no intellectual satisfaction in cleaning a bathroom. Celestine is so sharp. I'm hunting down employment that will satisfy her inner—"

"Stop," said Kirk Crick. "Celestine Amabo has never heard of job satisfaction. All she wants are walls to keep her family safe from murder, and food on the table. Let her handle her own life."

Mom listed the million things she was doing for the Africans and the million more she had planned. Kirk Crick, far from being impressed and wanting Mom to take over the world, said, "Back off, Kara. Celestine and Andre have to manage on their own as soon as we find them an apartment. You are encouraging them to cling."

This was Mopsy's cue. "Alake isn't even clinging," she said to Kirk Crick. "If I didn't make Alake eat, she'd starve to death as if she were still in Africa. There's something wrong here."

But Kirk Crick didn't stop talking, let alone listen. He acted as if he got a salary to yell at Mom for being a good person. By the time he left, Mom was trying not to cry.

How could Mopsy add to Mom's worries by pointing out all that was wrong with Alake?

Alake was Mopsy's responsibility.

♦

Sharing the bedroom was not as bad as Jared had antici-pated, although Mattu liked to count things—say, the number of shoes, boots, sneakers, sandals and socks Jared owned, and comment, "You have many possessions."

Like it was Jared's problem that Africa was dirt poor and peo-ple had to go barefoot.

What *was* his problem was that the bedroom had begun to smell.

Jared himself had smelly feet; he was used to smelly. But this was a different kind of smelly. Jared sniffed around, trying to lo-cate the source.

A day later the room had gone beyond smelly into foul.

"What's rotting in here, Mattu?" he demanded. "Don't look innocent. I didn't stink up the room."

Trapped, Mattu knelt in front of the long, shallow closet Jared had partly cleared out to give Mattu space. From the dusty back of the closet, Mattu drew out a dinner plate piled with the previous week's chicken and rice. There was no plastic wrap over the food.

"You can eat all you want, Mattu," said Jared finally. "But you can't store food in the closet. You have to store it in the refrigera-tor. That stuff is garbage now."

It was not garbage to Mattu. He did not surrender his plate.

"So here's the deal," said Jared, taking control of the plate. "We don't tell Mom you're hoarding rotting food in the closet. She'd go nuts that we might get rats or bugs."

"I have not noticed rats or bugs," admitted Mattu. "But of course they are here, eating their share."

"Don't say that around Mom!" yelled Jared. "I'm throwing this away, Mattu. You get hungry, you raid the refrigerator like a normal person."

◆

The next day was unseasonably warm. Mom took everybody into the village to have post office lessons, ATM lessons, library lessons and coffee shop lessons.

"Not me," said Jared. Throwing away rotted dinner had filled his whole charity slot. He was done with teaching refugees.

"I need you," said his mother, and her voice shook.

Mom never needed anybody. She was the toughest person he knew, tougher than Dad. Then he thought, She doesn't have Dad right now.

Jared was suddenly afraid. Suddenly aware that Dad wasn't ever home anymore. The house was so busy and chaotic that Jared had barely noticed how his own father was missing. Mom was carrying the whole refugee thing.

Mom drove down into the village and parallel parked, an art Jared yearned to conquer. He decided to ask Dad about driving lessons—dropping hints about how they needed Dad at home.

Or maybe not. Because what if Dad had reached his limit? What if he just couldn't stand any more of Mopsy dancing and

Jared moaning and Mom volunteering and Brady Wall stealing and crowds of Africans in need? What if Dad stayed away?

When they wrapped up at the post office, Mopsy wanted to show off the ocean. Jared would have driven to the town beach, a few miles away, where there was soft sand and picnic tables. Instead, Mopsy led them down a narrow lane between the antiques shop and the real estate office. All around were marinas, shuttered for the winter, hundreds of boats sitting up on props, shrink-wrapped in brilliant blue plastic. Even to Jared's eye, it was eerie.

Sticking out into the bay was a man-made breakwater—huge rocks dumped to make a wall about a hundred yards long. The rocks were very uneven, and at some point the top of the wall had been cemented over so that people who wanted to fish or walk out and admire the view had a better chance of staying upright. But salt water and New England winters were not kind to cement. By midwinter, the cement had rotted through and the rocks were icy and dangerous.

"In summer I like to swim off the far end," said Mopsy, trotting forward. "It's deep. Thirty or forty feet."

Alake refused to get anywhere near the water, never mind walk out on the wall. Mattu stuck his hand in the water. He gasped. "How can you swim in something that cold?"

"You swim in summer," said Jared. "It gets warmer." Actually, the water never got warm, just less cold.

Halfway out, Mopsy took a fall. Jared heard her knee whack the stones. She gave the kind of whimper that meant she wanted to sob but was trying to be silent and brave. She limped back. One plus—the Amabos were never going to get anywhere near the water again. They galloped back to the car.

When Mom started the engine, Andre watched longingly. He would never drive. Probably in Africa he hadn't given that a thought, but in America, where you vaulted into and out of the car every five minutes, Andre must have been painfully aware of what he would never do.

"The Nelsons are going to donate their old Honda," Mom announced. "Isn't that great? After you get your license, Celestine, you can drive yourself to work and pick the kids up at school and go to the mall on your own."

"I don't want to drive!"

"Nonsense. The grocery store is miles away. Your motel is even farther. We've got volunteer drivers, but they can't keep it up forever."

"No! I can't do it! I can't learn to drive. It's too much."

She *had* had to learn a million things already. Maybe learning to drive was too much for Celestine, at least this month.

"I know! I know!" cried Mopsy, clapping. "Mattu can be the driver instead!"

Andre and Celestine stared at Mattu as if they had not previously been acquainted.

"That is brilliant," said Mom. "Mattu—ready for a lesson?"

Jared came to a boil. If some refugee from Africa got to learn how to drive and was even given a free car, while he, Jared—forced to share a stinking room with him!—*didn't* get to drive...

I hate these people. I want them to leave and I want my father home.

But when his father did come home, Jared could not get him to understand how queer everything was.

"I'm over my head with the whole Brady Wall thing," said his father. "This is your mother's project. Just deal."

# CHAPTER SEVEN

THE DREAM NEVER CHANGED BECAUSE the truth never changed.

Alake stood with her slaughtered family on one side and the horrifying laughter of boy soldiers on the other. In her hands was a machine gun.

She loved her teachers. But she loved her sister.

Her sister's eyes were wide with fear and shock. Her teachers' eyes were wide with fear and shock.

*Do you want your sister to live?*

This was the choice.

Alake pulled the trigger. Her teachers were flung to the ground in a mist of blood. Victor took his weapon back. He was laughing. He shot Alake's sister anyway.

The most terrible thing about that terrible morning was that Alake no longer remembered her sister's name. Her sister's name evaporated like her town, for Victor left nothing standing: no people, no buildings, no animals, no crops. When he was done, Victor took Alake along.

She deserved whatever happened now, because she was as evil as any of them. She had killed two people.

Early that afternoon, they crossed paths with a convoy of

peacekeepers. Victor and the grown men with him melted into the bush. Alake and the boy soldiers were rounded up and taken away. What were the authorities to do with killers who were only eight or ten or twelve years old?

The killer children were isolated in a corner of a refugee camp, although the corner was not necessary. Everybody knew who they were. Not their names, nobody cared about their names, but what they had done. They were shunned. They could watch other children play. There were thousands of children, playing kickball and tag and soccer. But Alake and her group could not join in. Sometimes a boy tried, and then all the regular children would vanish and the child soldiers would be alone again.

Alone, they could not play. They did not know how.

Counselors came. We want to help you, they said. You are filled with grief and anger and shame, they said.

This was true, but the children did not respond. They were beyond help.

Once a missionary came.

Alake knew that she was a Christian, but even God was gone, without a trace, like her sister and her speech.

The killer boys had no women to pound their share of the grain, so they did it themselves, and after they made porridge, they left a portion for Alake. If they got rice, they gave her a share. Why? She was not really one of them; she had spent only a few hours in their troop.

After a long time Alake realized there was a school, and she crept toward it. She did not risk sitting under the shade of the awning with the regular children, children who deserved school. But because the teacher yelled every lesson so that students at the back of the crowd could hear, Alake also could hear. But she could not hold on to lessons any more than she had held on to her sister.

Alake was dead. It was just that she had a heartbeat.

Alake knew why Celestine and Andre were afraid of the dark. Celestine and Andre knew what was out there.

People like Alake.

♦

Yet again the refugee committee met at the Finches' house. Somebody had volunteered to take the Amabos out for the evening to see their first movie and taste their first popcorn. Jared wasn't sure this would work. Pizza had been a bust. Nobody would take a second bite. A seafood restaurant had been worse. Nobody would take a first bite.

Mopsy went along for the movie, filled with joy, of course, because it didn't take much with Mopsy, but Jared stayed for the meeting. He wanted to say what worried him, but he didn't want to sound racist or alarmist or just plain mean.

Mrs. Lame took charge, which depressed everybody, because she had so much to say about nothing. No surprise to Jared, she had been online and found a site where other African refugees were corresponding with each other. "When I took Andre to the doctor," she said, "I discussed the Internet and useful Web sites, but he simply would not pick up on it. I'm not sure how intelli-gent Andre is."

"Andre is sharp as a tack," said Mom. "It's not a question of intelligence. They've made it clear they don't want to deal with the past. Leave it alone."

Mrs. Lame was not the kind of woman who left things alone. "I printed out the best pages," she said, waving them around. "Celestine seems smarter than the others. I suggest you explain this to her. Furthermore, I'm worried about the daughter. What are we to do about this continuing silence?"

Perhaps the Mrs. Lames of the world were good for something after all. Now Jared wouldn't have to be the one to bring it up.

"Alake just needs time," said his mom.

In what way would time solve the problem that Alake's own parents didn't care about her?

But Alake was not of general interest. "According to my records," warned somebody, "at least four times a day, one of us is driving these people somewhere. When are they going to drive themselves? The days are turning into weeks and they don't make any progress. Where is the gas money coming from, anyway?"

"We have a separate refugee account, which was generously funded by the congregation," said Dr. Nickerson. "Intact," he added, before they could bring up Brady Wall.

"I think we should restrict clothing purchases to discount stores and thrift shops," said another person, which opened a heated argument. Did refugees deserve good, expensive new clothes, like the American kids, or were any old used clothes fine?

The apartment committee gave their report. They hadn't found anything. They didn't expect to find anything. Celestine was earning very little, and Andre nothing. The kids had to stay in school, so exactly how were the Amabos to pay for an apartment, not to mention food, a car and insurance?

Jared moved his chair next to Dr. Nickerson. It was the minister's excitement about sponsoring refugees that had stirred the congregation in the first place. Under the hum of Mrs. Lame's next topic, Jared said, "The way these four guys behave toward each other is creepy."

Bad approach. Instead of being appalled by the Amabos, Dr. Nickerson was appalled by Jared. "Their culture and lifestyle," said the minister predictably, "and the destructive qualities of war and long-term displacement in foreign countries have alienated them. It is our task to provide a warm, welcoming atmosphere in which they are not judged."

Implying that Jared was providing a cold, unwelcoming atmosphere and was judging left and right. Jared kept going. "They don't even seem to like each other."

"That's unusual? I have never noticed that you particularly like your sister."

"Right," said Jared, and he bailed. Mom and Dad were out, the minister was out, the committee was out. If things were wrong in this family—and they were—there you had it. Nothing Jared could do.

◆

"Where is Mattu today?" asked Mrs. Dowling.

"They're testing him in Guidance," said Jared.

Hunter leaned forward. "What did that African family do to deserve all this help? I don't see why refugees get to mooch forever and ever."

Only a few weeks before, Jared had fully agreed. Now he said cautiously, "I don't think it's mooching if we offer it."

"How come the church can't help inner-city people right here in America, who probably wouldn't mind a free car and job assistance?"

The church had had a lot of arguments about that. Luckily, those meetings had not been held at Jared's house. "Come on, Hunter. They suffered. It's okay for us to help."

"People have to make it on their own."

"They will," said Jared, who wasn't so sure.

"They'll end up on welfare," said Hunter. "That father, the one without hands. Who let him in?"

Jared felt an unexpected loyalty to his African family. Mattu was on Jared's team now, and Hunter—a friend since nursery school—was the outsider. Jared grew dizzy thinking about this.

"My ancestors got off the boat at Ellis Island," said Hunter, "and scrabbled and sweated and saved. That's what it is to be an immigrant."

Mrs. Dowling sensed a teaching moment. "Let's tell immigrant stories."

Half the class put their heads down on their desks to sleep

109

through this waste of time, but Tay said, "I have an interesting ancestor. My last name, Kinrath, is fictitious. The story is that my great-grandfather took syllables from the names of other people in line at Ellis Island and invented the name Kinrath. We don't know why he didn't use his real name, whether it was something slimy and horrible or something boring; whether he jilted a girl or murdered the mayor or just wanted adventure."

Jared was blown away. Tay's great-grandfather had faked his way into the country. Was it so terrible, then, if Jared's four Africans had done the same?

"Oh, come on," said Hunter. "Even generations ago, you had to have papers. You couldn't just say, 'I think I'll be Joe Kinrath.' So either your ancestor forged his papers or stole papers or—"

"Or who cares?" said Tay.

♦

The Refugee Assistance Panel discussed Victor's obsession with finding the strangers he had met on the plane.

"I think he wants this other family to support him," said Victor's caseworker.

"He hasn't gone to work since his first day," said the supervisor gloomily. "Is he asking for welfare?"

The caseworker was not sure that anybody's welfare was a priority for Victor. He said, "It's not our agency sponsoring the Amabo family. I could probably locate them, but I'd rather leave it alone. I've been telling Victor that privacy laws prevent me from getting that information. I keep thinking that once he realizes he has to support himself, he'll go to work after all."

The caseworker did not really think that.

He thought Victor was a dangerous man. But in America you could not go to the police about a person who had not yet done anything.

♦

Yet again the doorbell rang, and yet again the Amabos leaped out of their seats in panic. It was getting to Jared. This time Celestine knocked her coffee over. Mopsy went to Celestine's aid, Mom comforted Andre, and Dad looked as if one more visitor showed up in his house and he'd break china over their head.

So it was Jared who had to answer the door.

Because the side door opened into the garage, and because they generally kept the garage doors closed, theirs was a house where visitors mostly used the front door. Jared left the kitchen–family room, went through the spacious front hall, where the stairs curved so gracefully, and flung the door open. It never crossed his mind to see who was there first.

Big mistake. It was Emmy Wall. Crying.

"Oh, hi, Mrs. Wall," said Jared very loudly, to warn Dad. "Mom!" he yelled, giving Dad even more time to escape.

Mom rushed out of the kitchen. "Oh, Emmy! Poor you! Everything's so awful! Let me give you a hug!"

Jared sat back down at the table. If Mom had had a brain the size of a pea, she'd keep Emmy Wall out of the kitchen.

"Poor Emmy?" muttered his father. "Emmy's not poor. She has three-quarters of a million of our dollars. We're the ones who are poor."

"Emmy, darling, I'm just heating Drew's dinner. He's working such long hours and he got home so late. Let me fix you a plate too."

Dad stood up to leave, but he was too late.

"Oh, Drew," said Mrs. Wall, wiping away her tears, "I knew what Brady was doing. I kept thinking everything would just go away, but it didn't and now we're really in trouble."

"You knew?" shouted Jared's father. He slammed the four legs of his chair against the floor. "Emmy, you knew and you could have said something before it went this far? You could have told us or stopped him?"

Jared never wanted his father looking at Jared the way he was looking at Emmy Wall.

Celestine, Andre and Mattu were spellbound. Alake was stationary. Mopsy was sobbing in sympathy with somebody, but Jared couldn't tell who.

"He's a good man, really," said Emmy. "Drew, I know you're on the committee dealing with my husband. I want the church to give him the benefit of the doubt."

"He's got the benefit of three-quarters of a million dollars. Now he needs the benefit of jail."

♦

Mopsy was undone by her father's fury. "Come on, Alake," she whispered. "Let's go upstairs."

Alake obeyed. It was like having a windup doll.

In her room, Mopsy tried to calm herself by studying her nail polish selection. She chose a glitzy fire-engine red called Filmstar and put the first coat on Alake's nails. Mopsy could never wait long enough for her own nail polish to dry, but Alake never moved anyway, so her fingers just rested where Mopsy positioned them.

Mopsy had been dressing Alake daily out of Mom's closet, and while Mom's clothes were fabulous, they were not designed with a teenage girl in mind. Was Mom taking on the view of Andre and Celestine—that Alake was just silence on a stick and they could drape her in any old piece of cloth and who cared?

Mopsy cared. She dragged Alake into Mom's walk-in closet, moving slowly down the racks, flinging aside one hanger and then another. She chose a silky black and red shirt, and red suede pants. Mopsy couldn't imagine her mother even trying on red suede, never mind buying it.

Alake stepped out of her own clothes before Mopsy had to force her, put on the red trousers and buttoned up the silken shirt. Mopsy stood her in front of the full-length mirror.

Alake pivoted slowly, checking herself at every angle. Then, arching thin fingers over her head like a ballerina, the fresh polish glittering and a perfect match for the trousers, Alake lightly touched her hair and tilted her head questioningly at Mopsy.

*Alake was communicating.*

This was great, because Mopsy was sick and tired of silence.

The most fun thing in life was talking. "Hair is everything," she agreed. "Well, I guess not everything. I guess staying alive and having something to eat is actually everything. I've sort of gotten used to that train wreck on your head, but what you need is elegance. I totally see you modeling on a runway in a fashion show."

Then didn't Alake strut across the bedroom exactly like a high-fashion model. She swung her hips at an invisible audience, bowed to Mopsy's applause and sashayed off.

How could Alake know what a fashion show was? Andre and Celestine and Mattu had seen so little television they couldn't tell a cop show from the morning news, or car commercials from interior decorating shows.

On a shelf sat Mom's little wicker basket for mending. Its lid was open, and sitting on the neatly arranged spools of thread was a pair of sharp, dainty scissors.

Mopsy picked up the scissors. She marched Alake back into their bathroom, set the yellow ducky wastebasket in the middle of the floor and said, "Lean over this as if you're throwing up, Alake. I'm cutting your hair." Because after all, Alake's hair couldn't possibly look worse, only better. Mopsy snipped off the worst tangles and then snipped off the second layer of knots.

Alake put her thumb and first finger about half an inch apart and gestured toward the scissors.

"That's very short," said Mopsy dubiously.

Alake nodded, which was thrilling from the communication standpoint.

"Okay. It'll still be longer than Mattu's. You have a pretty head, Alake. It's like your face, bony and dramatic. You probably photograph very well, although in your picture from Africa I have to say you didn't look this good." Mopsy clipped happily. Maybe she would be a hairdresser when she grew up instead of a prosecuting attorney or a zoo veterinarian.

"Oh, Alake!" breathed Mopsy. "Look in the mirror! You are beautiful! I can't wait for everybody to see you."

♦

"We have homework," said Jared, glaring until Mattu tore himself away from the scene in the kitchen and came reluctantly after him. Up the stairs they went.

Voices followed them: Emmy sobbing, Dad yelling, Mom pleading for peace. It was like a representation of the world: one country paying for its greed, one country fighting back in rage, one country trying to stop them.

Jared could hear Mopsy cooing in her bedroom. Didn't she ever understand anything? Didn't she realize that Dad was coming apart this very minute, in this very house? That Dad was so close to smacking somebody—

Too close.

Jared changed his mind about how to handle this. "Come with me, Mattu. Whatever I say, you go with it. Got it?" Jared stomped back downstairs, planted himself in front of his father and said, in a voice that sickeningly resembled Mopsy's, "You know what, Dad? I had this brilliant idea. If we turn on the outdoor spotlights and light up the whole driveway, you can give Mattu his first driving lesson tonight. The sooner he can drive, the sooner they'll be independent." Jared took his father's hand, the way Mopsy ten times a day took Alake's.

Mattu was right on cue. "You mean it? I can start driving? Tonight?" he cried, as if he too had spent sixteen years waiting for this minute.

Jared scooped up the car keys and handed them over.

"I will watch," said Andre, moving to Dad's other side, and he and Jared swept Dad out of the kitchen, down the back hall, past the laundry room and into the garage.

Jared pressed the button to raise the automatic door and hit the floodlights.

"Why didn't you tell me these lights were here?" said Celestine, tagging along. "I would always want them on."

"I forgot," admitted Jared. "We like the dark so we can see the stars."

Dad showed Mattu forward and reverse, warming to the task because he didn't want dents in his beloved car and because he was a born teacher. A hundred yards backward, a hundred yards forward, Dad and Mattu traveled the driveway over and over.

Andre said to Jared, "You are a good son."

♦

Upstairs, Mopsy decided to do a test. She would parade Alake in front of everybody in the kitchen. Alake's stunning presence would give the three bickering adults something else to think about. And Mopsy would find out what it took to get Celestine and Andre's attention. They had not once acted like a mom and dad. Surely they would notice how terrific Alake looked in black and red. Surely they would admire the daring new haircut.

Mopsy headed for the stairs. "Come on, Alake. Let's show off to your mother and father."

Alake hung back. She looked pleadingly at Mopsy.

What am I doing? Mopsy thought. Tests are for school. I can't test Andre and Celestine, and I can't test Alake either. Home is where nobody tests you.

♦

Twenty-one days were left. He had to find the Amabos and get to New York City.

But Victor could not ask the refugee agency for help, because the only thing they could talk about was work. He had nothing to do all day except wander. He no longer had television, because the Sudanese men had been paying for the cable and Victor had paid no bills. He found bars where he could watch sports television.

Day by day his rage increased.

He considered torturing the resettlement staff, but they really didn't seem to know where the Amabos were. Once he telephoned the New York City number. No one answered. It was possible to leave a message but Victor didn't. Until he found the Amabos, Victor had nothing to sell.

# CHAPTER EIGHT

THE AMABOS HAD BEEN LIVING with them for more than three weeks when Mom turned on the TV and the weather forecast was for snow. "It's about time," she said. "We're having such a wimpy winter." She couldn't look out the windows, because they were covered as if in a wartime blackout, so she flung open the back door to put her face right into the wind. Then, with difficulty, she slammed the door on the gale. She was drenched by rain. "I guess it isn't snowing yet," she said, laughing. "It'll turn to snow during the night. Is anybody's bedroom window open?"

Celestine and Andre would never dream of opening a window. Alake's fingers never touched anything, that the Finches knew of, and Mopsy liked her room cozy (stale, in Jared's opinion). Only Jared was a big fan of fresh air. His windows were always open. He trotted upstairs.

He had forgotten Mattu's boxes of ash.

Water had blown in and pooled on the wide window shelf. The bottom of each precious box was dark and buckled.

Horrified, Jared slammed the window down. There was no way to pretend this had not happened. Why did he have to be in charge of refugees and their stuff, especially disgusting stuff like dead people's ashes?

It seemed reasonable to move the boxes to a dry place. Jared lifted one and the bottom fell out. The cremated remains of a grandparent slopped around in a gritty puddle. Jared even got bone mud on his fingers. He wiped them off against the dry top of the box. The cardboard was so weak that this ripped the side seam, and the rest of the contents spilled onto the carpet.

Jared turned on his desk lamp to illuminate the extent of the disaster.

The bone pieces that were still dry were gray and irregular like gravel. But the wet bone bits gleamed. They were pretty. In fact, they were enchanting, which did not seem like a quality bones would have.

Jared forgot to be queasy. He picked up the largest wet piece. It puzzled him. Wouldn't bone have a sort of perforated look? Wouldn't it be all but weightless after cooking in a fire? Jared held his wet pebble up to the lightbulb. A streak of color and fire shot out.

It's a diamond, thought Jared. A rough diamond.

Jared ran his fingers through the bone mud. Mattu had smuggled uncut diamonds out of Africa. Dozens of them.

♦

Victor discovered coffee shops. There he could sit for hours in air-conditioned comfort, sipping coffee and watching people.

Many customers spent their time staring into folding computers and typing on tiny keyboards. Victor asked for a demonstration. The person he asked was so fascinated by his own computer that he did not even look up. "Sure," he said, scrolling through the front page of a newspaper and clicking through sports and a celebrity video and a piece about the war zone in the Middle East. He threw a smile in the general direction of Victor. "You can find anybody or anything on the Internet," he said.

"You can find people?" said Victor.

"Easy."

"I do not have a computer and I do not know how to use them."

"No problem. Go to the library. The computers are free. The librarians do it for you."

♦

Jared had definitely never imagined playing in dead people's ashes. If that was what this was. More likely, Mattu had scooped some ashes up from some old campfire, and calling them "my grandparents" was a brilliant lie by a clever smuggler.

Jared smoothed away the fingerprints he had left in the mud.

The pebble—or raw diamond—or weird shiny glowing bone—was oddly warm in his palm. He slid it into his jeans pocket and ran downstairs.

Everybody was in the family room.

Celestine was working hard on her new hobby—clipping

grocery store coupons, which she studied constantly, drawing up new and exciting shopping lists. She loved the arithmetic of whether canned tuna was cheaper at Super Stop & Shop or the Food Mart. She was eager to save fifty cents here and twenty-five cents there. Every day she came home from scrubbing toilets and asked when that unknown wonder, her paycheck, was going to arrive. Would she do that if she knew she had a fortune in diamonds?

Andre was watching an old basketball rerun. Jared couldn't stand the thought of sports that were not happening right this second. It made him crazy to look at ballplayers in weird old-fashioned shorts and tight little shirts and worthless sneakers. But Andre, who would never hold a ball again in this life, was breathless with excitement, rooting for the team he'd chosen. In his lap lay the precious piece of paper from the medical center with the date and time of his next doctor's appointment. Andre loved those appointment sheets. Would he love them that much if he knew he had diamonds?

Yes, because having hands was better than having diamonds. So Andre might actually know about the diamonds. Yet when Celestine read her grocery list aloud, Andre looked up, bright-eyed and eager. Vegetables! he seemed to be thinking.

Was he also thinking, And when we cash in our diamonds, we'll buy an estate in the country and a great car, and we'll eat all our meals out?

Jared couldn't see it.

Alake was just too screwy to be included in diamond smuggling. Although with the fabulous new hairstyle Mopsy had given her, she looked intelligent and thoughtful instead of lost and dumb.

Alake was sitting next to Mopsy, who was deep in a teaching moment, reading aloud from her favorite picture book, trying to make Alake say *"Tyrannosaurus rex."* Alake was not saying it.

Mattu was sitting on the floor in that squat/crunch/posture nobody but baseball catchers could achieve. His lips moved as he read his biology textbook. He did not hear or see the television; he was not aware of Mopsy's silly story. He was completely absorbed in the page, treating every word like gold.

... or diamonds.

If they all knew about the diamonds, wouldn't they be more of a team? Jared could imagine them saying to each other, We're out of here. You be the son, you be the daughter, we'll be the grown-ups. We'll get to America, cash in our diamonds and lead the good life.

But why would anybody choose Alake? And if you were planning all that, wouldn't you rehearse? Wouldn't you at least coordinate escape stories?

It was a mystery. But in some ways, all families were mysteries. Maybe even all people. Look at the mystery of Brady Wall. He had turned into a completely different—

*Turn in,* thought Jared.

Diamonds or no diamonds, papers or no papers, Jared could not turn his family in.

Because somehow, the Amabos had become his family.

One summer, Jared had gone to camp on a lake. There had

been swimming and canoeing and water polo, but what he remembered most was that he forgot his family existed. His whole life was camp. When his parents and baby sister showed up on Visitors' Day, he was shocked. Who were these people?

The people who mattered lived with him at camp.

When you lived with somebody, they mattered.

Jared cleared his throat. "Mattu, I left the window open and rain blew in. It soaked into your boxes. I tried to move them to a dry place but the boxes split. I'm really sorry. We have to transfer the ashes into new containers."

Did this announcement have an impact on anybody? Celestine's pencil was no longer moving over her grocery list, but maybe she was done. Andre gasped, but it could have been at the game. Mattu's eyes grew huge, but they did this fifty times a day. Alake was always motionless anyway.

"The ashes of your grandma and grandpa?" shrieked Mopsy. "Oh, Mattu! This is so awful!"

Mom, always practical, said, "Tupperware, maybe? Until we buy real urns?" She threw open the cabinets and produced two round plastic containers with bright blue lids while Mopsy got the DustBuster.

"No," said Jared. "You can't vacuum it. You'd mix the ashes with dust and lint." Not to mention, he thought, that the pebbles, which might or might not be diamonds, are too heavy and wide to go through the slot.

♦

It's my fault, thought Mopsy. I weakened that box. What if I have to admit it? What kind of disgusting person goes pawing around in somebody's grandparents' ashes?

They all swarmed upstairs after Mattu, but when Mattu reached Jared's door and saw the mess, he put out his arm to block the Finches. "This is my responsibility. Please wait downstairs. Thank you, Mrs. Kara, for the new—" He blanked.

"Tupperware," said Mom, as if it were a password and now she'd get to stay.

Had Mattu been calling her mother Mrs. Kara all along? Mopsy hadn't noticed. There was so *much* to notice that she didn't notice *enough*.

Reluctantly, everybody left Mattu alone with the ashes of his grandparents.

Downstairs, Celestine was now adding a column of numbers, using her favorite new toy, a tiny purple foam calculator. Andre was cheering his team. Mopsy was never going to understand cheering a rerun. Those were Andre's parents up there in a puddle. Shouldn't he react a little more than this?

When Mattu finally rejoined them, Mopsy had a hundred questions. "What happened to your poor grandma and grandpa, anyway, Mattu?" she began.

"They were clubbed to death."

She had not expected an answer like that. Maybe she hadn't even expected an answer. She was nauseated by the physical closeness that clubbing meant. The killer's eyes would have looked into the victim's eyes. The person trying to flee would have watched his killer's fingers tighten on the stick. You'd have to pack a lot of muscle into the swing of your club to commit murder. What had the club been made of? The only club Mopsy had ever seen was used in golf. She blundered into the next question. "Was it the same day you got your terrible scar?"

"His scar is not terrible," said Mom, who liked to pretend that awful things were just fine fine fine. "Mattu is a very handsome boy."

It occurred to Mopsy that marriage to her mom must be annoying. Mom could never allow anything awful just to be awful. Mopsy looked at her father. He was staring down into his cell phone, no more aware of dead people's ashes than Andre was. Mopsy stopped caring about Mattu. What was she going to do about her father?

"Mattu, you're shivering," said Mom. "Here. Have a blanket."

They all had their own couch blankets, two or three yards of fat cushiony fleece. Dad, who was always hot, and Jared, who was always hotter, never touched their couch blankets, which stayed neatly folded year after year. Mom and Mopsy, on the other hand, had favorites.

Mattu accepted a huge length of scarlet, which he flung grandly around his shoulders, a tribal prince in royal robes. Alake not only watched him, she actually looked back at the couch blanket pile. Mopsy picked out her personal favorite, a swath of hot pink, and wrapped Alake like a package.

Alake wore her blanket to the dinner table.

"No," said Mom. "You need your hands to eat, Alake, and

you're going to eat tonight. I'm sick of you not eating. Give me the blanket."

"Hang on, Alake," said Jared. "I've got this big thick sweatshirt I never wear because I hate it. It's perfectly acceptable for dinner-table wear, and it's just as fleecy on the inside."

Mopsy knew what it would be: the mauve Metropolitan Opera sweatshirt Grandma had given him for Christmas. Jared would die before being seen in it. When he came downstairs and tossed it to Alake, Mopsy said, "I don't think it's a good gift if it's something you hate, Jared. I think a good gift has to be something you love."

Alake caught the sweatshirt, pulled it over her head and adjusted it around her shoulders.

"Don't get all philosophical on me, Mopsy," said Jared. "Alake likes it and it solves the problem. And now when Grandma asks if I love the sweatshirt, I can say yes. I just won't add that I love it on somebody else."

◆

It *was* love.

Alake loved the softness of the fleece on her skin. She loved the color, sort of like the raspberries that even Mrs. Finch, who would buy anything, refused to buy because they were out of season and too expensive.

Alake loved how the sleeves hung past her fingers, so that her terrible hands were hidden even from her. In a way, she envied

Andre. If her hands were gone, would the murder she had committed with those hands also go away?

♦

After dinner, Celestine did not return to coupon study. She read a book: the Bible. It was Jared's, actually; the one all kids got in fourth grade, when people figured they could read for real. This Bible was a version called *The Message*, and it had never crossed Jared's mind to open it. It had been gathering dust on the bookcase near the sofa since fourth grade.

Dad was still just sitting, now and then rubbing his forehead or eyes.

Celestine said softly, "It hurts that your friend took from the church."

Jared could tell by his posture that Dad simply could not bear to talk about this anymore with anyone.

"This thief worked at your side," said Celestine, "pretending to work with you, but in fact, working for himself. The loss of money hurts the church, but the broken trust hurts you."

Shock sliced through Jared like a machete. *He, Jared, was a thief.* He had stolen from Mattu. And broken a trust, because he was only pretending to work with Mattu.

His mouth was dry.

I didn't steal anything, he told himself. It was just there, I just looked at it, I just held it up to the light to see what it was. *And didn't put it back.*

Emmy Wall had sobbed the very same words. *Brady meant to put it back. He didn't mean for anybody to notice, because he was going to put it back.*

Am I going to put my diamond back? Why did I take it, anyway?

What would Mattu say to Jared when they were alone in the bedroom?

But that night Mattu fell asleep as usual, his even breathing filling the room. Maybe he hadn't counted the diamonds.

Maybe they weren't diamonds.

Around one in the morning, Jared slipped out of bed, crept down the stairs and slid into the kitchen–family room. Shutting the doors so nobody would hear the soft clicking of the keyboard, he turned on Mom's computer, went online and did a search.

"Diamonds" and "Africa" gave him plenty of hits.

He found a site about diamonds in South Africa's famous deep mines with their tight security and followed a link to diamonds in West Africa, Mattu's side of the continent.

Here, diamonds were alluvial, which meant they lay near the surface of the earth, spread by streams and seasonal rains. They were dug up with plain old garden shovels. The "mines" in Sierra Leone were actually fields, and diamonds were the crop.

Those diamonds paid for, and had started, and were a big reason for the continuation of, Africa's many civil wars. Diamonds bought guns and machetes, jeeps and uniforms, food and drink. Diamonds turned ordinary men into killers. The killing was not part of a plan to change a government or society. It was just killing. The diamond guys liked to shed blood, so their source of income was called blood diamonds. West Africa—Sierra Leone in particular—was the source of most blood diamonds.

Some sites didn't say "blood diamonds" but "conflict diamonds," which made the gems sound like the source of mild arguments, whereas *blood* diamonds implied the slash in Mattu's cheek, and his dead grandparents, ruined sister and handless father.

One article insisted that in Africa, any government activity required a bribe. The best bribe was solid money rather than paper. That meant gold or silver, or in much of Africa, diamonds.

Jared had never bribed anybody for anything. He was confident his parents never had. Teachers bribed students all the time, of course—If you're good, you can go to the auditorium for the presentation on diving for underwater treasure, they'd wheedle. But even when you weren't good, you still got to go, because the teacher wanted to go too.

Okay, so bribes. Maybe the Amabo family had bought their way out of Africa.

Jared always worried about those boat people from Cuba or Haiti or wherever. They wanted what the Amabos wanted: food on the table and the safety of walls. They were willing to do what Celestine was willing to do: anything. Willing to do what Mattu was: go to school, study hard.

Jared just could not reconcile the behavior of the Amabos with blood diamonds.

I've been watching too many movies, he thought. The family says these are ashes, so that's what they are.

He tried a few more sites, looking for specific information about West Africa. He was reading the very paragraph he'd been hunting for when somebody breathed next to him. Jared practically had a heart attack. But it was only Mopsy. "What are you sneaking up on me for?" he demanded in a whisper.

"I want to talk," she whispered back. "What are you doing?"

"Studying up on Sierra Leone and Liberia and all."

He expected Mopsy to say, I might believe you'd be up in the middle of the night checking baseball statistics, but you're Jared; you're not down here studying scary little countries in Africa. Instead, Mopsy nodded. "Because Andre and Celestine and Mattu and Alake are not a father and mother, a son and a daughter."

His bouncy little sister, who was not known for thinking at all, had come to the same conclusion he had, when their mom and dad hadn't. "I agree. I don't think these four people are related."

"I think Celestine and Andre go together," said Mopsy. "Think about what Celestine has to do for Andre in private. Would you do that for some stranger? Now tell me what you found out online."

Jared pointed to the screen. "West Africans don't usually cremate people."

Mopsy nodded. "Did you look in those boxes?"

"Yes."

"Stuff glows."

"I saw." He reached into his pocket. The stone had a silky feel. "I took one," he told his sister. He could not believe that of all the people he knew, he trusted *her*. "I think they're raw diamonds."

"Take it to a jewelry store and ask," said Mopsy.

# CHAPTER NINE

THE AFRICANS WERE UP AT dawn to see what snow was like. Eight inches had fallen. Andre waded in it, poking the stubs of his arms down into the snow and flinging the white stuff around. What was it like, Mopsy wondered, to feel things without fingers?

Mom dragged out a big cardboard box of mittens and scarves and a huge clear plastic container of boots. Everybody gathered around to examine this unfamiliar gear.

"Oh, look!" said Mopsy happily. "My baby mittens." They were attached by a long crocheted cord, which threaded down her sleeves and over her shoulders so she wouldn't lose them. "Usually," Mopsy explained to the Amabos, "that's for little kids."

"Or me," said Andre eagerly.

Celestine and Mom took an old pair of Dad's gloves, made a hole in the leather of each with an awl, strung a cord through and looped the cord over Andre's shoulders. When Celestine helped him into Dad's old winter jacket, gloved hands appeared at the bottom of the sleeves.

The snow was heavy and wet—perfect for snowmen. Jared and Mopsy and Mattu rolled a ball until it was so large they couldn't move it any farther. They made the second snowball, packed it hard and carefully lifted it on top of the base. The third, smallest ball took only a moment. Mom handed out celery, a carrot and prunes, which became green hands, orange nose and wrinkled eyes, and a scarf Dad hated anyway and would be happy to find ruined.

The Amabos gazed upon this snowman with more than their usual fascination and puzzlement.

"Is it part of your religion? asked Mattu.

♦

While the others were making a second snowman, Jared went inside for breakfast. It was a school day, although doing so much so early in the morning made it feel weekendish. There sat Alake in the yellow and cream living room, lost among the sofas, not even looking out the windows at the snow.

Jared felt a strange rage. He grabbed an old ski jacket of his own—so weird dressing a girl his age—and pushed her out the door. She didn't join the others. Nor did they call to her.

Jared escorted his mother inside. "How long are you going to let this go on?" he snapped.

"Let what go on?"

"There's something so wrong with this family. And with you too, Mom. You're lavishing all this care on Mattu and Celestine and Andre but you're pretending Alake isn't alive, just like her own mother and father do. Celestine and Andre figure Alake is dead in heart, and if just they wait long enough, she'll die in body too."

"That's disgusting," said his mother. "Don't you be negative and unchristian to Celestine and Andre, who are doing their very, very, very best. I believe that with love and comfort and counseling, Alake will be herself again one day."

"And have you seen Celestine and Andre offer any love or comfort to Alake?"

But the back door opened and in came Celestine, Andre and Mattu, and they were all carrying snowballs and had not kicked the snow off their boots and Mom rushed forward with a new set of important American rules. She did not notice that all three steered around Alake.

Celestine made waffles (she was in love with the waffle maker) and heated up the syrup (she was in love with the microwave) and fried the bacon (she was way better than Jared at flipping the package over to check the little bacon window for fat). She had discovered place mats, folded napkins and candles. It was a very heavily decorated breakfast table.

Dad hated this kind of thing. He liked breakfast without adornment. Just put a piece of toast in my hand and let me run to my car, was his motto. Where was Dad, anyway? He couldn't have gotten up any earlier than Andre. Was he hanging out in his room, waiting for people to leave?

Jared texted his father. *miss u where r u?*

"Eat fast," said Celestine. "You have to catch your bus."

"I can't eat fast," said Mopsy. "I don't know how. I'm a slow eater." Carefully she buttered her waffle so the exact right amount of butter melted in each little square.

Celestine and Mom heaved identical sighs.

How strange was the structure of this new family of eight: Celestine adored and wanted to be just like Mom, while Mom loved molding Celestine in her image. The two of them were surging forward. Andre, as if attached by his mitten cords, was not lost and floating but learning everything, poised on the edge of a life in which he too could participate; a life with hands.

Maybe it was Dad who was lost and floating.

Dad answered the text message immediately. *Left early.*

I'll say, thought Jared. He read the rest of the message. *Hold the fort i lv u.*

Jared poured syrup on his waffle. A minute earlier, he'd been ready to tell Dad about the diamonds. But the message troubled him. Maybe what Jared needed to do was *empty* the fort instead of holding it. Drew Finch had to earn a living and support everybody and their hobbies. He was required to save the church, the world, a man without hands and a girl without speech. Did he really need to worry about smuggled blood diamonds as well?

And even that was a guess. Why give Dad another burden that might not even exist? Jared had to *decrease* the demands on his father. God, help me out here, he prayed. How'll I do that?

"Jared, darling," said his mother, as if she were God, answering. "I think Alake's had enough middle school. She needs to go to high school with you and Mattu."

Jared said to God, Come on. I wanted *you* to handle it.

God waited.

Jared sighed. "What do you say, Alake? Want to be a junior?"

Alake could have been a photograph of herself, for all the response Jared got.

"Great. That's settled. Come on, Alake."

♦

In the guidance office Jared explained who Alake was, and that she hadn't talked yet, and that her records, such as they were, were at the middle school, and asked whether Alake could come to class with him for the day.

Nobody commented on the fact that Alake's supposed brother had gone straight from the bus to that same class without helping his supposed sister get registered. Of course, now that Jared thought about it, any normal brother would wear dark glasses and adopt an alias before he'd help his weird younger sister enroll.

"Hmmm," said the guidance counselor. "I think since Alake is a girl, we need a girl escort. Bathrooms and stuff. How about Tay? She's in your first two classes."

Tay was not only out of Jared's league, she was a million miles from the crazy silent world Alake inhabited. "Sounds like a plan," said Jared, who figured the plan might last twenty minutes.

Tay was summoned. She bounded in so full of zest that Jared was reminded unpleasantly of Mrs. Lame. Tay flung her arms around Alake and kissed her on both cheeks, while Jared repeated Alake's history for her. "What a privilege. Wow, what a dramatic haircut, it looks fabulous on you. Don't worry about the whole not-talking thing, Alake, I talk enough for both of us." Tay turned her smile on

Jared. He was immediately hypnotized and willing to spend his life at her feet. "See you in class, Jared. We're hitting the girls' room first."

In American history, Mrs. Dowling had returned to the subject of Internet communication with other refugees. Speaking clearly and loudly, she explained again to Mattu how the Web worked. "I have found several sites," she said, enunciating carefully, "—a site, Mattu dear, being a specific place online where you find information—where people from Africa who have come to America try to find relatives. This will get you started." She held out a sheaf of papers.

Mattu stared straight ahead. "You are kind. But I have too much knowledge of the past. I do not want the past to follow me. Please do not continue in your effort."

Mrs. Dowling stuck the papers in his face. He did not take them.

She set them down on his desk. He folded his arms across his chest.

Several kids snickered.

Jared had a feeling that nothing good could come of this. Mrs. Dowling had offered a gift and Mattu had publicly rejected it. Mrs. Dowling was one of the mean ones, blind to her own cruelty because of her conviction that she was one of the nice ones.

Tay waltzed in. "Ladies and gentlemen, this is Mattu's sister, Alake. Eat your hearts out, because *I* am her assigned escort. Kelsey, shove over. I need your chair for Alake."

"Where am I supposed to sit?"

"My lap," said Hunter.

*"Eat your heart out?"* Mattu whispered to Jared, horrified.

**137**

"Just an expression. It means, I bet you're jealous of me now." Jared had to laugh. Mattu so visibly could not imagine being jealous of anybody saddled with Alake.

"Alake has chosen not to talk," said Tay, "so don't expect feedback."

Chosen? Jared had never considered that possibility.

"Mattu, what happened to your poor sister?" everybody said, aghast and curious and pushy.

Mattu stiffened.

"Leave him alone," said Jared. "He just told you the past is too awful to talk about. I read online about this region in Africa called Darfur? And not only do thirty percent of the people from Darfur live in refugee camps—almost two-thirds of them watched somebody in their family get killed. That's probably what Alake went through. She'll be fine one of these days," he added.

He couldn't imagine why he had said that. That was Mopsy's line, or his mother's. Jared did not believe that Alake was going to be fine.

♦

A few classes later, Alake once again sat next to Tay, who used her finger to point out each word in the book she held. The students were taking turns reading poems out loud, finding the rhythm, leaning on the rhymes.

The poem Tay read was about a horse traveling through the

woods in snow. Alake had just encountered snow. She had never seen a real horse, but she had looked into New England woods for almost a month now.

*"The woods are lovely, dark and deep,"* read Tay.

*"But I have promises to keep,*
*And miles to go before I sleep,*
*And miles to go before I sleep."*

The poem was beautiful. Now the miles ahead of Alake seemed a little less frightening. She could almost imagine traveling on, although she could not believe that she would arrive somewhere lovely, dark and deep. The words echoed gently in her mind, comforting her.

Tay bundled Alake on to gym, where the girls were playing basketball, which Alake had seen on television, because Mr. Finch and Andre liked it.

The gym teacher put an arm around Alake. "We're going to do some exercises, class. Alake and I will do them together." With Alake at her side, the teacher ran lightly and easily around the court. She bounced the big orange ball in a steady rhythm, with the flat of her hand. When it was Alake's turn, it was harder than she had expected. But how vibrant the ball was, as though it loved bouncing and yearned to sail through the air.

The class divided into four teams and played two half-court games of basketball at the same time, while Alake and the teacher kept circling the perimeter, dribbling.

When Alake was little, she had known the meaning of hospitality. Her family had taken everybody in. That was the reason for a dwelling: to take people in. They slept in your rooms and you gave them gifts when they departed, and knew that soon you would visit them.

Hospitality had been killed by the civil war. The only people who came during war were the killers.

Now Alake was in the midst of hospitality again. A family had opened its home, its beds and its refrigerator—what a marvelous thing the refrigerator was. A church congregation had opened its doors and supplied clothing and food and jobs and doctors. A school had opened its classrooms, and now this girl, Tay, had opened her arms, and so had the gym teacher, and even the basketball.

The gym teacher cried, "Good job, Alake!"

At dinner, the American parents asked their children what they had done all day long, and no matter what the children said, the American parents cried, "Good job!" Teachers cried, "Good work!" Counselors, "Good choice!" Even the art teacher had exclaimed, "Good color!"

And of course, the minister talked about good too. But the minister meant something else; something Alake was not and could never be.

The high school lunchroom looked just like the one at middle school, except bigger. Tay walked to a table where girls shifted chairs to let Alake and Tay sit together. Alake was puzzled by their laughter, which seemed to have no cause.

They were welcoming her.

Alake could hear them. She could see them. She sat carefully in a chair. She could feel its chilly plastic. She could smell the soup they were eating. *She was alive.*

Jared dragged over a chair from another table and sat down. "Come on, Alake. Eat something. It's a sandwich, is all. It's good."

Jared is good, thought Alake. All the Finches are good. They are so innocent.

Imagine a house where you do not even have shutters to bolt at night. A house where you laugh if you forget to lock a door. A house without weapons.

I want to be happy like these girls, thought Alake. I want to chatter the way they chatter, and have a friend. I want to sleep without nightmares and eat without gagging.

"Good job," said Tay, when Alake lifted the sandwich. "Now bite down."

Alake wanted to breathe the snowy, chilly air. To read with Mopsy. To do arithmetic. Drive a car. Fill brown paper bags with groceries.

She wanted not to be evil.

She had been twelve years old. Now she was a thousand. She could never get those years back. She would be a thousand years old as long as she lived.

The walls of the cafeteria were covered with student art projects in a thousand colors, like the church with its color-shot windows. That church where they spoke of forgiveness. But Alake could not be forgiven for the things that she had done.

She put the sandwich down without eating it.

♦

In the last class of the day, Mattu was dressed for gym and out of the locker room before Jared had even undone the snap on his jeans. Jared's jeans were perfect now, because he'd been wearing them for five days. He hated that first five minutes when his freshly washed jeans were all crisp and irritating. He always had to go into protection mode to keep his mother from snagging the nice soft jeans and throwing them into the laundry. He peeled off the jeans and threw them toward a locker, and something fell out of his pocket and skittered across the tiles.

Hunter bent down to retrieve it for him and then laughed. "You collecting gravel these days?"

The diamond. Jared had gotten used to its tiny bump. He hadn't even remembered it was in there. His mother could have found the diamond if she'd gotten hold of his jeans. Would she know what a rough diamond was? It was always difficult to guess what his mother might know. She was a combination of totally out of it and totally aware.

Hunter took aim at a distant trash can, threw the pebble overhand and made the basket. Cheering himself, he jogged out of the locker room.

I don't even know yet if it's a diamond, thought Jared. But if it's lost in that trash, I not only don't have it, I can't put it back.

I'm Brady Wall, he thought.

His tongue felt dry and swollen. His heart felt old and creaky. He upended the trash container and kicked the contents around the floor. The assistant gym teacher came in. "I fell over it," said Jared. "Don't worry, I'm cleaning it up."

"I'll help," said the guy, which was the last thing Jared wanted. Then he saw the pebble under filthy gym shorts somebody had probably thrown out rather than lugging them home to wash.

It was warm and familiar in his hand. It was a diamond, he knew it was.

♦

Mrs. Dowling sat at her home computer.

Poor Mattu was in need of friends. His own kind. People who would understand him. Mrs. Dowling could not trust a lazy slug like Jared to use her careful research. And poor Mattu was superstitious about the Web.

Mrs. Dowling took action. She compared the various sites she had turned up. She chose the most active. Then she posted a kind and detailed description of Mattu Amabo and all she knew of his family.

# CHAPTER TEN

IT HAD NOT OCCURED TO Mattu that he might love his American family. He was grateful and he ate their food, but he had not planned to love them.

The skinny, rushing, constantly talking mother had been so tiring at first, with her relentless pushing and doing and her countless activities. But the minister and the church committee faded away, while Mrs. Finch continued to believe that all problems could be conquered, all hurt souls rescued and all hands reattached.

The father was gone so much, working to pay for this amazing house and the family's cars and computers. He was visibly sad and exhausted. But when Mr. Finch was home, he offered his good suits and ties for Mattu to wear in church and patiently gave him driving lessons.

How clearly Jared hated sharing his room, his friends and his time. But it was Jared who watched out for Mattu, tutored him, even stepped in to protect him. As if Mattu—fresh from a world where you needed a submachine gun to defend yourself—cared about some minor bully like Hunter. Jared was reaching out even to Alake, who could not—should not—reach out herself.

But the real reason Mattu loved his American family was

Mopsy. This little girl completely adored the four strangers who had invaded her house with their problems and demands and secrets. When Mopsy spun and danced and clapped over nothing at all, Mattu could almost hear his mother's laughter, back when there had been joy.

He loved the Finches. But how he had ached to be among black people. He was so glad to be at a restaurant with Daniel's family, who had the same color skin he did. And what a family: the mother a college professor and the father a doctor. He wished he could be alone with them, instead of saddled with Alake, Celestine and Andre.

The restaurant was filled with fresh flowers, bright colors and soft seats. The food was arranged like art. Mattu had expected Daniel's family to be like everybody else but more so—blasting him with questions about Africa and his past, refugee camps and suffering. He'd been wrong. Conversation was entirely about the future: Celestine's future, Andre's, Mattu's—even Alake's.

"Daniel is hoping to be a doctor. He's more interested in research than in patient care. Mattu, have you thought about what you want to be?" said Daniel's mother, leaning forward with the same intensity Kara Finch had.

I want to be safe, thought Mattu.

He did not try to explain. She was talking about careers and education. Mattu did not want these beautiful people to know the depth of fear and horror that slept with him by night and engulfed him by day.

Celestine was not sharing Mattu's thoughts about safety. She was actually looking at him the way a mother would look at a son . . . a son who could become a doctor.

Daniel's father smiled. "Is it too soon to plan the future, Mattu?"

Mattu smiled back. "The present is enough for now. I am behind in every class. But I will catch up."

"What's your best class?" demanded Daniel's mother.

"I am not best at anything. In every class, I am at the bottom. There are not always schools to attend when a country is at war. I am deficient in many fields."

"But what do you *like* the best?"

Doors that lock. Trees that don't hide killers. Plates with food on them. "Math," he said politely.

♦

Finding the library took several days.

The librarians could not have been nicer. They located ten agencies that were licensed to settle refugees in America, but they found no clues about Victor's dear friends, the Amabo family. "We'll keep working on it," they assured him when the library was closing for the night. "It's a challenge. And how exciting that we may be able to reunite you with your friends."

♦

"Celestine has her first checking account," Mom told Kirk Crick. "She chose checks with a background of wild animals.

Would you believe that even though Celestine is African, she has never seen leopards or tigers or elephants? We're thinking of going to the Bronx Zoo this weekend to make up for that. Meanwhile, Alake is now going to the high school, where she has a wonderful buddy assigned to her, and wait till you see her beautiful hairstyle! And we're having such fun with brand preference. They all know the difference now between Pepsi and Coke, Burger King and McDonald's, whole milk and skim. Celestine prefers mint-flavored floss. Andre prefers hazelnut-flavored coffee."

Jared hadn't known about any Bronx Zoo trip. There was an area of Manhattan called the Diamond District. If he could get Mom to change her plans and take everybody to the Empire State Building, which was also in Manhattan, he could take off and go into one of those shops and get his pebble identified.

The other afternoon he had actually stood on the sidewalk in front of Prospect Hill's jewelry store. Its windows were filled with necklaces shining on white velvet throats and engagement rings gleaming on black velvet trays. But the salesgirl inside looked only an hour or two older than Jared, and he didn't think she would even have heard of rough diamonds, let alone been able to identify them. And did he really want to be asked right here on Main Street, a block from his church and half a mile from his school, just exactly how he had come by an uncut diamond?

It crossed Jared's mind that he might not be the only one in this house who would like to find the Diamond District.

Kirk Crick sighed. "You're treating the Amabos like household pets, Kara. Your task is to give them a boost and shove them out, like birds from a nest. All your projects are way too much. It isn't good for them. They have to do this stuff by themselves."

"They can't even drive yet. How are they supposed to do anything without me? They can't get to the store or the bank in the first place unless a church volunteer drives them."

The aid worker shrugged. "Public transportation."

"There isn't any," Jared pointed out.

Kirk Crick put his Amabo folder back into his briefcase. "Then I'll find them an apartment some other place where there is. I'll be back next week."

"It isn't time yet! There's still so much to do!" cried Jared's mother.

"Look, Kara," said Kirk Crick, heading for his car. "You're the innkeeper. People stay with you *temporarily*. The good deed is helping them leave."

♦

On Sunday, Alake sat beside Mopsy and they shared a hymnbook. The music poured over her like cool water soothing a fever. She loved the hymns and the enthusiastic singing of the congregation. Her feet and heart shivered from the pipe organ's volume.

"The Lord be with you," said the minister.

"And with you also," said the people.

And had that happened? wondered Alake. Was the Lord with these people? Was he also with her?

*"Open my eyes, that I may see,"* said the first hymn.

Alake prayed as she had never known a person could pray. Open my eyes! she begged God. Let me see you the way other people see, not through the veil of the bad things I've done.

*"Open my heart,"* said the hymn. *"Open my mind."*

Oh, God! Open my life, that I may be part of this!

*"Silently now I wait for thee,"* said the hymn.

Not that, Lord. I don't want to be silent. I want to talk.

The room seemed full of answers. If Alake just dared to stretch her fingers, she could catch hold of a word—two words—even an answer.

But people in this church did not stretch or leap or dance or cry out.

They sat quietly.

♦

Sunday afternoon, the entire Finch family seemed exhausted. Mr. Finch napped in front of the television. Mopsy fell asleep leaning against her father. Jared fell asleep playing a video game. Mrs. Finch dozed over her knitting.

Alake felt brave. All by herself she would go to the bedroom she shared with Mopsy. Americans believed you could start over. Americans believed that even someone like Alake could be a new person with a new future. She would look into that mirror and see if there were any traces of what she had prayed for: her new self, cleansed of all that had come before.

Alake walked slowly up the stairs. She dared pray to that God, the one who forgave.

But down the hall from the other direction came Andre. Andre had never looked at her, and he didn't look at her now. He knew who she was; they had all known, at that camp.

She was someone not worth speaking to, not worth looking at. Someone who had killed.

If Alake had ever had a message from God, this was it.

You cannot escape what you did, God said to her. Africa is in this house with you. See what Victor's soldiers did to Andre's hands? It cannot be undone.

You cannot be forgiven.

◆

The librarians came through for Victor. They found the information he needed. They were happy about it. So was Victor. Where, he asked them, was this place called Prospect Hill?

They printed a map. They printed driving instructions.

"Is it as far as New York City?"

"Farther. It's past New York. Maybe a hundred and fifty miles north."

Victor took his maps and left. Driving required a car. Victor went out on the streets to get one.

♦

The snow melted and then froze again that night, coating the roads with ice. Trucks threw brown sand in a lacy pattern, but the hill was still treacherous.

Icy weather was a signal to Mom that cookies must be baked. Jared thought this was a nice habit in a person. He stole a little dough while Mom was showing Celestine the cookie cutter selection.

Dad was giving Andre and Mattu a map-reading lesson. The Amabos didn't come from a world with enough paved roads to bother with maps. Maps were difficult. Andre was struggling to figure out which little lines on the local map were the ones on which he'd ridden his bike.

"And these?" Celestine asked Mom.

"Easter shapes," Mom explained. "That's a bunny and that's an egg."

"How do you celebrate Easter in Africa, Celestine?" Jared asked, guessing that Africa had a real shortage of Peeps candy chicks and plastic grass.

Celestine slid her first batch of cookies into the oven. To Jared's amazement, she actually answered a question about her past. "Last Easter, in the refugee camp, when many children had died of diarrhea, there was such sorrow. But we were joyful that Easter was coming."

"Excuse me?" said Jared. "How could you feel joyful when babies were dying?"

"Because Christ is risen and he is with us in our suffering. On Easter morning, I was at peace over the death of my daughter."

Mopsy stopped reading.

Dad stopped looking at the map.

Mom stopped rolling out dough.

"We had another daughter," explained Andre softly. "She is in heaven. We do not talk about her."

So Alake was just a throwaway kid—the daughter who had survived. Her parents resented her for being alive. There was no rescue from that.

♦

Victor returned to the little apartment to get the various things he had acquired. Some of those were weapons.

The refugee supervisor was waiting at Victor's apartment for Victor to appear. "You made promises when you were accepted for refugee status," he said to Victor. And then he made a fatal error. "You promised to work and to hold a job. If you are not at work tomorrow, I will have to call Immigration about you."

♦

Celestine and Mattu stood with their backs pressed against the garage, as if they expected to be shot.

"Oh, my God!" Dad kept yelling.

Jared's father never swore. Jared couldn't imagine what had happened.

Dad was so mad he was panting. "Driving back and forth on our driveway is not enough practice for you to take the car, drive across town and get on the highway! You have to have a license, Mattu! What made you go to Stop and Shop anyway? We couldn't fit another Cheerio in this house. And you can't just take my car! Did you hit anything?" he shouted, clearly envisioning streets full of dead toddlers, smashed cats and dented school buses.

Mattu and Celestine exchanged horrified looks.

They *had* hit something.

Please don't let it be anything formerly alive, thought Jared.

"A grocery cart," whispered Mattu. "When we drove away. It was just there. In the middle of where you park the car. It stuck to us. I couldn't get rid of it. Finally it rolled off."

Jared began laughing hysterically.

"I wanted to work at that grocery store instead of the motel," said Celestine desperately. "I telephoned for a job interview, just the way it said to do in our manual."

"This is fabulous, Daddy," said Mopsy. "Taking the initiative and testing abilities and exploring unknown territory. It's like a checklist for life. Did you get the job, Celestine?"

"I start Monday," she whispered.

"Congratulations!" shrieked Mopsy. "I'm so happy for you! Even though I would rather be dead than a checkout clerk."

"I'm a stock person. I'll put things on shelves. Things to eat."

Mopsy flung her arms around Celestine and they kissed and

hugged. Dad pulled himself together and patted her shoulder. Then he informed Mattu that driving lessons were over.

"I, on the other hand," said Jared, "am mature in comparison, and ought to be the one taking driving lessons."

"Good plan," said Dad. "The way I'm feeling now, any time I can drive away from here is a good time."

"But right now," said Mom, "it's dinnertime. My schedule always trumps your schedule."

"So true," said Dad glumly.

Everybody paraded into the kitchen, which is always a family's favorite room and which in this household was really and truly the favorite because that was where all the food was.

Jared was the last to leave the frigid garage and the only one who saw Alake. She had not been part of the action or part of the result. Nobody had hugged her or even thought of hugging her. Maybe hugs were more crucial than food. But Jared couldn't hug her either. "You okay, Alake?"

It was a stupid question.

But she did not treat it stupidly. She looked at Jared with real eyes—the eyes of a person. Sad eyes.

♦

They were home alone, Alake and Mopsy.

Mopsy had a plan. She always had a plan for Alake. She had dragged out another old picture book and was reading aloud to Alake, poking her finger at each word. Inside her fleece blanket,

Alake was shivering with pride. She could read every one of those words by herself. Everything she had learned in Africa, before life went wrong, had come back into her mind. She could read!

Mopsy turned the page. There was a picnic under a tree, and there were happy children with wide curved smiles. Alake had a sudden beautiful memory, untainted by blood and evil: her family, smiling, under a tree.

An ugly rasping sound came from outdoors. Like a motorcycle, but rougher. Alake stiffened.

"It's not our car," said Mopsy. "It's somebody who needs a new muffler and probably everything else." She ran to look out the window. "It's all rusted out and beat up," she reported to Alake. "And old. Longer and flatter than cars are now. Plus an ugly color. Who would drive that thing?"

Alake stood up. Her couch blanket fell to the floor.

She followed Mopsy into the front room, keeping her back against the interior walls and making sure she was not visible from the windows. She rushed to the drapes and looked carefully through the crack. She gave a little moan of horror and then sprang into the front hall before Mopsy could. Every night Celestine double-checked the front door to be sure that the upper knob, which moved a fat metal bolt into the frame, was turned in the right direction. The safe direction.

It wasn't turned. The door was unlocked.

Alake shoved the dead bolt home.

♦

Mopsy was sick of being patient with Alake. "It's okay," she said. The pointless anxiety was driving her crazy.

The doorbell rang.

Alake fled upstairs. Mopsy could tell from the sounds that Alake had gone not only into the bedroom, but into the closet.

Mopsy opened the door for the stranger.

Mopsy loved strangers. They were so much more interesting than people you already knew. Uncovering the details of other people's lives was Mopsy's specialty. In fact, now that she thought about it, probably being a talk show hostess was her best future.

"Hi," said Mopsy, smiling. "Are you here about the Amabos?"

# CHAPTER ELEVEN

JARED AND MATTU WERE ON the late bus. Jared was sleepy in the overheated bus.

Mattu asked suddenly, "What do you think it means in church when they say your sins are forgiven?"

"It's a crock," said Jared, not bothering to open his eyes. "I don't believe there's such a thing as sin anyway. Just look at television. You can do anything you want with anybody you want for any reason you want and what happens? Nothing. There are crimes, and sometimes people go to jail for them, but not always. I bet Brady Wall gets off."

"But if they chop off your hands, have they not committed a sin?"

All these Africans had to do was utter one sentence and all Jared's thoughts were flung into turmoil. Yes. There were still sins. And chopping off somebody's hands was one of them.

Mattu said in a low, intense voice, "Could you be forgiven for chopping off somebody's hands?"

Jared wanted to leap off the bus and walk home. Had Mattu chopped somebody's hands off? Andre's, for example? No wonder these people didn't talk to each other.

"Would Jesus forgive?" Mattu pressed.

This was so not Jared's thing. "Ask my parents." He felt queerly out of breath. Panicky.

"It is your thought I wish to hear."

"I don't see how even Jesus could forgive somebody who chopped off somebody else's hands. It would be like forgiving the Holocaust."

"What is the Holocaust?" Mattu asked.

Jared was always startled at how little Mattu knew of the West. But why did Jared have to be the person to explain? One good thing. Jared had learned that he was not destined to be a teacher. One future career down, a thousand choices to go. "This nightmare that happened in Germany in the 1940s. The bad guys penned up several million Jews and slaughtered them. It's called the Holocaust."

Mattu nodded. "We have those in Africa. I have been in one."

♦

George Neville had been so tense at Kennedy Airport as the Finches left with the Amabos that he had hardly even noticed the little Finch girl. He was pleased that she had recognized him, although how hard could it be, since he was probably the only black person she'd ever met before the Amabos got here?

Mopsy brought him a plate of sugar cookies, gleaming with pink and white icing. The cookies were delicious.

"Celestine made them," the little girl told him. "There is absolutely not one thing that Celestine can't do. She got herself a new job too. On her own. She's amazing. And Mattu just found out that a boy at high school—Ian—has an after-school job. Mattu didn't know there was such a thing. He went to work with Ian yesterday, and they can take Mattu on too, and he starts next week."

This was excellent news. George had been worried about this African family, and even more worried about their American hosts. It hadn't been extra work but a relief when Kirk Crick had called and asked if George could make the weekly visit this time. "How is Mr. Amabo doing?" he asked, remembering the sad, cringing father in the stretched-out sweatshirt and the sight of those naked arm stubs.

"Super. He and Mom have gone for the final visit to the surgeon before the first operation. You would not believe how fast everything has come together. I was worried because I thought he was going to get hooks, but they'll tackle the one cut off closer to the wrist first, and if it works, it's going to be an actual hand. Would you like to see photographs of the technology?"

"I'll pass, thank you. And how's the daughter?"

"Alake's upstairs. I'll run and get her. She has the most fabulous new hairstyle. I cut her hair. I did an awesome job, if I do say so myself. Although my mother had to clip a little bit more on one side where I got it lopsided. Alake's going to high school with Jared now, and her escort is Tay, so everybody is jealous, because who wouldn't want Tay walking around with you?" Mopsy headed for the stairs.

Through the front door came Mattu and Jared, shaking off snow and laughing. "Hey, Mr. Neville!" cried Mattu. "Great to see you again!"

♦

Upstairs, Mopsy said severely, "Stop hiding from people. People are nice. He's your refugee guy. He isn't going to deport you or something. Is that what you thought, when you recognized him?"

Nothing was going to make Alake head downstairs while Mr. Neville was here. Which was just as well. No need for him to find out that Alake was still silent.

Mopsy thought up some really good lies to tell Mr. Neville about why Alake wasn't trotting down to show off her new hairstyle, but it turned out not to be necessary, because just then Celestine was dropped off by her church volunteer driver, and Mopsy knew, because it happened with everybody, that even Mr. Neville would not think of Alake again.

Mopsy flung herself onto her bed and caught sight of her computer screen on the way down. "I know what let's do. Now that you're in high school, Alake, I never see you, and I never know what you're doing. I'm going to show you one more time how to send e-mails, and then you're going to write to me and that's that, Alake. I can totally tell you can read now, because out of the corner of my eye I was watching your eyes move from word to word when we were looking at that book. And the real bonus is, you still don't have to talk. E-mail is perfect for you." Mopsy shoved Alake onto the desk chair and propped her hands on the keyboard.

Alake studied her fingers as if they were objects on a shelf.

"Type!" shrieked Mopsy. "Or I'm going to start kicking you. Communicate with me!"

A tiny smile seemed to quirk the corners of Alake's lips. She lifted her hands. Curling her fingers just as Mopsy did, she began to tap letters. One by one, letters appeared on the screen.

Mopsy caught her breath. Okay, God, this is the time. Show Alake she's a real person, and make her figure out that real people talk to other people.

But the letters on the screen were random.

They did not form words.

*deerjopsyeilovyouo*

Alake was not trying to communicate. She was just tapping.

Mopsy told herself that they were making progress; at least Alake's hands weren't lying in her lap like stuffed animals. And typing was new to Alake—this was her very first keyboard moment. Mopsy should not have such high expectations. Still, it was depressing. Quinnie said Alake couldn't do anything. Mopsy had been hoping she could saunter into school and say "Alake can *so* do anything."

Alake's posture was strange. In fact, Alake seemed to be the one holding her breath. She looked at Mopsy, and she seemed to want something. What?

Mopsy looked at the letters again. *deerjopsyeilovyouo*

*Dear Jopsy.*

*I love you.*

Mopsy began to cry. "No, don't change the 'J' to an 'M.' It's perfect the way it is. You were just up one row when you aimed at 'M.' I love my new name. Now what we're going to do is, we're going to forward your first-ever message to Quinnie so she knows you've named me Jopsy."

On the screen, Mopsy opened her address book. She clicked Quinnie's name. The message space appeared. Mopsy typed standing up, her arms in Alake's face. *Here's Alake's first e-mail. Isn't this great? I'm still Martha to you, but I'm Jopsy to Alake. Write back immediately so Alake gets into e-mail and does it all the time.*

Alake elbowed Mopsy away from the keyboard.

This was the best thing to happen in weeks! Mopsy thought. This was true communication. This was how sisters behaved. They shoved.

Mopsy was totally happy until Alake deleted the name Quinnie and painstakingly typed in *Tay*.

Even though Mopsy adored Tay and wanted to be just like her when she grew up (assuming she ever did; all bets seemed to be against it), she didn't want Tay to be the important person in Alake's life. Mopsy wanted to matter most. She sighed but called Jared on her cell phone to demand Tay's e-mail address. "Stop lying, Jared. You do so have it. You just don't want to share with me.

I know Tay texts you during the day to let you know how it's going."

Jared sighed so loudly you could hear him ten telephones away. Then he dictated Tay's address and Mopsy typed it in.

♦

The body of the refugee supervisor was discovered in a parking lot. His hands had been cut off. The amputations, said the coroner, had occurred before the man died.

The murder made the news in Texas.

But not in Connecticut.

♦

Mr. Neville was long gone, and Jared and Mattu and Alake were downstairs watching television when at last there was a message on Mopsy's e-mail. "Alake!" she screamed. "Get up here! Tay answered! It's addressed to you, so you have to read it!"

Alake went up the stairs like a shot, like a real person who really and truly wanted to say real things. She tiptoed into Mopsy's room. She seated herself carefully in front of the computer. She straightened her clothes.

Because it's important, thought Mopsy. She has written to Tay and Tay has written back.

Alake read the words, Mopsy could see by her eyes. But just in case Alake needed backup, Mopsy read it out loud. "Dear Alake, this calls for a celebration. I have just the gift for you. I'm on my way. Love, Tay."

♦

But of course the first car to pull in the driveway had to be Emmy Wall's.

Mopsy moaned, printed out Tay's e-mail, handed it to Alake and skittered down the stairs to open the door. "Hi, Mrs. Wall. Mom will be home soon. Alake and I were just going to make hot chocolate. Want some?"

Alake was halfway down the stairs, holding her e-mail the way the Magi must have held the baby king's treasures. She wants to share it, thought Mopsy. But she doesn't know how.

Mopsy led the way into the kitchen.

Under normal conditions, no grown-up would ever want to sit in the kitchen and chat with a sixth grader and a mute African. But Mrs. Wall was desperate. She and Alake sat at the kitchen counter on the tall stools while Mopsy prepared the hot chocolate.

Jared yelled, "Make enough for us!"

Mopsy yelled, "Make your own!"

Since Jared and Mopsy were actually only a few feet away, the yelling was not necessary, except that for brothers and sisters it was always necessary.

The doorbell rang again. But this time, it was not Alake who almost fell off her stool. It was Mrs. Wall. "I'm scared it'll be the police," she quavered. "They want to question me."

"On TV, the police can't come in unless the homeowner lets them," said Mopsy. "I'll be the homeowner. So they can't come in. Anyway, it's probably Tay. She's got a present for Alake. Alake, you answer the door. I'm stirring. The chocolate will burn if I stop."

Alake gave Mopsy a very readable glance, which said, Are you insane? I'm not answering the door.

But since they had not locked up after Mrs. Wall arrived, the visitor came right in.

"Alake," said Tay, "needs somebody to love. And sometimes a puppy is easier to love than people."

♦

Except for vicious slinking mongrels even hungrier than she was, Alake had never encountered dogs in Africa. She did not like dogs. But the orange and brown and white puppy Tay put in her arms was different. How cuddly and warm the puppy was! Its big brown eyes stared into hers. Its little tongue licked her palm.

It had been years since Alake's arms had encircled another living being. Warmth from the puppy seeped into Alake's heart.

"We have four collie puppies," said Tay, "and we have to give them all away."

Americans had so much. They gave away food and clothing, houses and cars, kisses and hugs—and now puppies.

"Aren't the puppies valuable?" asked Mopsy.

"No, because we aren't sure who the father is. So they're

probably not really collies. But this little guy looks like his mother."

Alake did not know if she looked like her mother. She never would know, because there had never been photographs. Alake shifted the puppy until they were both comfortable. The puppy licked her. Alake buried her face in the puppy's fur.

"This is going to work," said Tay. "Let me get his blanket and bowl from the car and you are all set."

"Wait," said Mopsy. "My mother will say no, because since Zipper died a few years ago, she hasn't wanted another dog."

Already the thought of losing the puppy was appalling. Alake began to cry. The tears were hot on her cheek. Her heart began to beat faster. She could actually feel her blood pumping. Her fluids were coming back. Hope floated on the surface. The puppy licked her tears, which was silly and fun, and Alake wept more on purpose.

"Don't cry!" shrieked Mopsy. "I'll talk Mom into it, Alake, I promise. After all, this isn't our dog. It's yours. You can have the puppy. Don't cry!"

♦

The Texas police could not locate Victor. This was in part because the photograph they had—the one on his paperwork—was not in fact of Victor.

The interstate had already taken him out of Texas. The car seemed to fly. The impossible two thousand miles seemed possible after all. He drove through the night. When he needed gas, he waited in the parking lot of a huge roadside restaurant and gas station. He was waiting for a woman with a pocketbook. She put up a fight but not enough of one. Victor used her credit card for the gas.

The interstate was a separate world, like the airplane. But on the plane, Victor had had no control. On the interstate, he controlled everything.

♦

Mattu listened to the house, always so full of sound: the hum of its machinery, Mopsy practicing her flute, Jared singing along to his iPod, sports announcers shouting on the television, Mrs. Finch laughing on the phone, Mr. Finch clattering lightly on his computer keyboard, the wind and weather outside.

Whenever Mattu listened carefully, he found that he also smelled carefully: the scents of cleansers, the deodorants of which the family was so fond, the last breath of Mopsy's tuna fish or peanut butter, the flowers Mr. Finch liked to bring his wife, the cinnamon sprinkled on the buttered toast.

"We need to talk," said Celestine very softly. "Let us go for a walk."

They had never talked. Mattu felt a shudder of excitement. He and Celestine were going to do what the Americans wanted them to do: plan for the future.

The day was mild by Connecticut standards but still

shockingly cold to Africans. Celestine put on her puffy new coat and her fat slickery mittens. She looped a long wool scarf around her neck and pulled a knit cap down over her ears. Mattu huddled in his layers. Jared never covered his head or ears with a cap or scarf, and neither did the other boys at the high school. Mattu, however, had found a huge fake-fur hat with earflaps in the church donation box. Jared refused to associate with him when he wore it.

They went down Prospect Hill and into the village. The piles of recent snow here and there were grimy and ugly. The sidewalks were slippery.

"Here is what matters," said Celestine. "My husband is going to have hands again. Or at least one hand—they are relatively sure they will succeed with the right hand. They can fix the mechanism to his wrist and teach him to use the plastic fingers."

"Will they be white fingers?" asked Mattu.

"No. They will match his skin color exactly."

"This is an amazing country."

"And I will not have our future ruined," said Celestine. "You must find Victor. Get the diamonds to him."

Mattu stopped walking. The thick jacket did not keep him warm. The heavy hat did not protect him. He could not look at Celestine. He could not look anywhere. Fear lodged in his spine, between the bones, right where a knife might lodge.

"Victor will not work at some ordinary job," said Celestine.

This was true. Victor had no skills. Well, actually, he had

plenty of skills—he could drive a jeep, point a machine gun, murder children and torch houses.

"He will want one thing only," said Celestine. "His diamonds. At the airport, when I realized that we were ahead of him, I thought we could disappear if we moved quickly, and then somehow we were attached to the Finches and there was no way to disappear, and yet we got here, and I thought, Maybe we have disappeared after all. When you study those maps, you see how huge this country is. How tiny and hidden this town is. But Victor will never give up."

Mattu stared down the narrow lane where Mopsy had led them the day of their post office lesson. He could see a tiny slice of the little harbor, the cold water gleaming in the weak sun. On the other side of that water was Africa. It seemed impossible.

Also impossible, Mattu had nearly forgotten Victor.

Victor had been one of the killers who ran the refugee camp—the officials only thought they ran it. But there were factions and gangs inside the camp just like inside any other prison.

Some family of four had been next on the list of refugees to go to America. Their name was Amabo. But they refused to cooperate with Victor. They were going to America, they said, and Victor could rot. He could beg all he wanted, but they were flying away. No, they were not going to help him.

People did not win arguments with Victor. He did not argue. He killed.

Victor took the Amabos' papers and found four people to take their places.

People who were afraid, like the husband and wife who became Andre and Celestine. Victor explained that if the husband did not cooperate, he would lose his feet as well as his hands.

People who were helpless, like the girl who became Alake.

People who would do anything to get to America, like the boy who became Mattu.

The boy knew what Victor had done to the real Amabo family, because everybody except the officials knew. Those people are dead anyway, the teenage boy told himself. I can't help them. But I can get to America.

He was used to the name Mattu now, although he had not planned to keep it. He was used to Celestine and Andre. Nobody could get used to Alake.

Victor had passed out any number of diamonds to accomplish his exit. But the hard part was yet to come. He had to enter America. Diamonds did not show up well in X-rays and were not detected by metal detectors. Nevertheless, Victor had not wanted to carry the diamonds himself. A single man in his twenties was always suspect, whereas a family of four would find sympathy. A single man in his twenties might have anything stashed inside the boxes he carried and would receive a thorough search, whereas a girl grieving for her grandparents, a girl thin and wasted and sad—the silly Americans would offer her comfort and not check everything.

But Alake's fingers and face did not respond to Victor's orders. When he told her to carry the boxes, she failed him. He could not hurt her because the paperwork was for four people, including a teenage girl, and the plane was shortly to leave, and he needed her. So it was the boy who had to carry Victor's boxes.

The plan had been for the five refugees to land in New York and get past the officials. Then Victor would take his diamonds to the dealer who had promised to buy them, and whatever happened to the fake Amabo family would happen. But it had not worked out that way.

"He made it your job to deal with the diamonds, Mattu," said Celestine. "Now you must finish it. Find him before he finds us. Take the diamonds to Victor."

No, thought Mattu. I can't. I won't.

"Do not let him follow you when you leave him," said Celestine.

But maybe Victor had slid into being American the way Mattu and Celestine and Andre were sliding—at high speed, with no brakes, stunned and gulping but thrilled and cooperative. Maybe Victor had turned over a new leaf and was busily earning money and using a stove and admiring vegetables.

And maybe not.

"If he follows you," said Celestine, "you cannot come back here. Not ever."

♦

Jared had been reading up on raw diamonds.

For use as jewelry, a rough diamond was cut at angles, which created the facets that glittered. Diamond cutting was difficult and risky. If you cut wrong, you ended up with diamond dust instead of a valuable gem. Most diamond cutters were in certain cities in Europe, such as Antwerp. Some merchants were in New York. Some traveled back and forth, buying in Africa and selling in America or Europe. Diamond cutters weren't supposed to purchase blood diamonds. If a person wasn't sure about the background of the rough diamonds set in front of him, he wasn't supposed to buy them. An unethical diamond cutter bought good rough diamonds no matter what.

Jared stared at his possible diamond and considered the other thief in their lives.

Brady Wall was in jail. He had not been able to raise money for bail because he had stolen from the only people likely to help him in a pinch. There was talk about whether Emmy Wall would go to jail too. She had not stolen. But she had known.

The Walls didn't have kids. But from his first marriage, Brady had had two children, one a year younger and one a year older than Jared. Church youth groups included a wide range of ages, and when Jared had been in the middle school group, so had both of the Wall kids. They lived with their mom now, and she had remarried and moved away.

If Jared had been a good person, he'd have e-mailed them and said something nice. Like what? In spite of the fact that your dad's a felon who steals from churches and gambles hundreds of thousands of dollars into the ground, I hope you're doing fine and you like your new school.

I'm a thief, he thought. The only difference between me and Brady Wall is, I haven't gotten caught.

He went upstairs to his bedroom. Mattu was in the shower. Mattu could not get over the amount of water that was available to the Finches. He was still impressed by the faucets, and how they never ran out, and how you could have icy cold or burning hot water any time you wanted; how you could press a glass against the fridge door and get ice cubes or frosty water or ice chips. He loved carrying a bottle of water around at school and he loved sipping from the water fountains and he especially loved taking showers.

Jared opened one of the Tupperware containers and dropped his diamond—or haunted bone—into the ashes, popped the lid back on tight, gave the thing a little shake and stepped away.

He was still a thief. But he had put it back.

♦

Since Alake did not talk, she did not pick a name for the puppy.

"It's bad enough having a puppy," said Mom crossly. "I'm not having a puppy I can't even yell at!"

Mopsy took Alake's face in her hands and turned it toward her. Staring into Alake's eyes, she said, "Name. The. Puppy."

Alake said nothing.

"How about Jopsy?" said Tay. "I think it's just right for a collie."

"Here, Jopsy," said Mom.

The puppy ran right over, not because he knew his name, but because Mom had a dog treat cupped in her hand, left over from when Zipper was alive. It looked like magic.

But maybe puppy love was magic, because Alake's face was bright in a way Mopsy had never expected to see.

♦

The mere thought of finding Victor brought Mattu close to vomiting.

Victor wants to be rich in America, thought Mattu. That's why he needs the diamonds. He wants a house like this, and cars and computers and clothes. Suppose Victor wants these diamonds to pay for more war in Africa? Or what if Victor wants to use the diamond money *against* America? Victor would not care what war he fought. People who liked violence found each other.

But in Africa Victor had been a person taking advantage of war, not a person with convictions and interests and politics. Mattu did not think Victor had ever had a plan for or against America. He had planned only for himself.

Now it was Mattu who needed a plan. A way to get rid of the diamonds that didn't lead to Victor's getting rid of Mattu.

I was a coward once, thought Mattu. We all were. I could have turned Victor in instead of taking the place of some dead boy.

But in fact, nobody could have turned Victor in back at the refugee camp, because Victor just bribed his way past and around and out. Another diamond, another step toward America.

174

It was a ludicrous position for Mattu to find himself in—heavy with diamonds, desperate to be rid of them, unable to do it.

Mattu stayed in the bathroom until he heard Jared go downstairs. Then he lay down on his bed, the softest bed he had ever known—in fact, the only soft bed he had ever known. After a while he forced himself to look at the Tupperware containers.

Little rocks worth a great deal of money. Mattu knew how many dollars were in a gallon of milk and how many dollars were in a gallon of gasoline, but he had absolutely no idea how many dollars were in an uncut diamond.

A diamond seen through an airport X-ray machine did not cast a shadow. Yet a blood diamond always cast a shadow: the shadow of death.

Wait! thought Mattu, sitting bolt upright. George Neville said Victor might be going to Texas. I've seen Jared Google. I'll Google. Keywords like "Texas" and "refugees." "Texas" and "refugee aid societies." "Texas" and "African refugees." I can find the agency that sponsored Victor.

Wild with excitement, Mattu flipped open his laptop.

Then he sagged in despair. So what if he did find the agency? Only words crossed the Internet. Diamonds had to be carried. There was no getting around the fact that Mattu would have to hand the diamonds in person to the man he least wanted to see in this world.

Mattu was living in a house full of snoops and going to a school where attendance was taken in every class. Texas was half the country away. How could he get there? And what about the money required for such travel? Not to mention the real difficulty—if Mattu did find Victor, Mattu would die. Victor didn't let people go. Mattu would be buying a safe future for Celestine and Andre, and ironically, for Alake. But what about his own future? The one Daniel's mother had outlined? The one high school was preparing him for?

Mattu prayed to the God the Finches worshiped—almost but not quite the same God Celestine and Andre worshiped.

I want school, he prayed, and that part-time job and the apartment of our own and also to get rid of the diamonds and the past and Victor.

I'm already an American, thought Mattu. In Africa, you pray for one meal. In America, you pray to have it all.

Mopsy yelled upstairs, "Dad rented movies and he's heating chocolate sauce for ice cream. You need a break, Mattu. It's so hard on a person to do homework, don't you think?"

How American, to think schoolwork was hard on a person. Mattu went downstairs for rich, thick vanilla and caramel ice cream with hot chocolate sauce, served in his favorite small, heavy red bowl.

Mrs. Finch ruined everything by opening a can with a disgusting smell. It was not the kind of smell Mrs. Finch normally allowed in her home.

"What is that?" asked Mattu.

"Dog food." Mrs. Finch spooned some out, put it in a bowl and set the bowl on the floor for Alake's puppy.

Mattu could not puzzle through one more crazy American habit. He fell into the cushions next to Mopsy, and when the movie began, he fell into the action as well, so there was none of him sitting on the couch and all of him inside the film, and he forgot Victor again.

♦

A few feet away, sitting at the kitchen counter, Mrs. Wall and Mrs. Finch talked softly.

Alake sat on the floor next to them, stroking the soft, sweet ears of her puppy. He had a whole separate smell from the dog food, a warm, furry smell. He was exhausted from his big day, and when he finished his supper, he crawled contentedly onto her lap.

"You come to church with me this Sunday, Emmy," said Mrs. Finch. "Sit beside me. I'll tough it out with you."

"No. I'm going back to Wisconsin."

"*Wisconsin?* You've lived here twenty years!"

"And now I'm leaving. I can't face people."

This made sense to Alake. For three years, Alake had been among the people she had wronged, and never once had she faced them. Had never looked up, never spoken. She wondered where Wisconsin was and whether Mrs. Wall could face people there.

*Dear God,* prayed Alake, *help Mrs. Wall.*

Alake felt God listening.

Her prayer actually traveled to God, and he was glad to hear from her.

Alake looked carefully at Mrs. Wall. Will I be able to see God helping her? Will it be in her eyes?

The puppy whimpered, sensing that Alake's attention was not fully on him. Alake buried her face in his wonderful fur.

♦

Jared listened to his mother and Mrs. Wall.

He had had a sort of argument with Tay in school while they were waiting for their respective Africans to finish up at the guidance office. "I don't see you guys in church anymore," he had said casually, because he would have loved to see her every day of the week.

"We don't go anymore. My parents are furious about that theft. They gave their hard-earned money to the church and what happens? A deacon steals it. Church is supposed to improve people, but it obviously doesn't."

Jared was not sure that self-improvement was the purpose of church. But he said, "My parents are furious too."

"People who go to church are such hypocrites," said Tay. "They dress up in their fine clothes and carry their matching handbags and plump down in some pew and sign up for committees and pretend to be religious, but really they just want the attention."

Jared had often laughed at his mother's need for handbags that matched all her outfits. And of course she loved attention. Who didn't?

But she signs up for committees hoping to do good in the world, he thought. She believes that's what God expects of her. She believes.

"But nobody believes any of that stuff anyway, not for real," said Tay.

My mother does. Andre. Celestine. Maybe Dad. I'm not sure about Dad. He's so shaken. And me? What about me?

♦

"Don't pack for Wisconsin yet," insisted Mrs. Finch. "Come to church Sunday."

"Impossible," said Emmy Wall.

"Possible," said Kara Finch.

That is the difference, thought Alake. In Africa, everything is impossible. But in America, everything is possible.

# CHAPTER TWELVE

THE PUPPY HAD A SOFTENING effect on everybody. Even Dad kept saying to Alake, "Talk to your puppy. Jopsy has to get to know your voice." Jared thought the puppy might do a better job of keeping Dad home than his wife and children were doing.

Alake looked ready to talk. But she couldn't quite get there.

"Jopsy has to learn to sit, stay and heel," Dad told her. "But above all, he has to learn not to beg. You feed Jopsy one more time from the dinner table and you're both sleeping in the garage." But he was smiling when he said this. And it seemed to Jared that a smile trembled on Alake's lips too—that she was ready to be happy.

When the doorbell rang, for once the Amabos did not act as if someone had thrown a grenade. But it was Kirk Crick, and he had in fact come with a grenade.

"I've found an apartment," he said briskly. "It's in Norwich. Forty-five-minute drive northeast of here. Nice and cheap, because Norwich is a depressed little city. The apartment's not very big and it's not very clean, but we can get volunteers to help scrub and furnish it. The high school, the Norwich Free Academy, is excellent. There's another Super Stop and Shop there, Celestine, and I've already called the managers and they're happy to switch you to that location. Mattu, I can't do anything about your new part-time job, but you can hunt for another one. The important thing is, Mattu will have his driver's license soon. With the donated car, the Amabos have their own transportation, and that will give them real freedom. The current tenants are moving out today, and we can get you in there by the middle of next week."

Celestine glowed. Her jaw was set at a determined angle and she sat straighter.

Andre lifted sparkling eyes. His lips moved as he thanked the Lord.

It occurred to Jared for the first time that a refugee must hate being a refugee.

Who wants to be on the receiving end of charity? Nobody. And in their own home, no matter how sad the city or how shabby the space, the Amabo family would not be refugees.

"They're not ready!" cried Mopsy.

"It's like learning to swim," said Kirk Crick gently. "If somebody always holds you up, you never learn. But once you're in over your head, you start paddling."

"Or drown," said Mopsy.

Kirk Crick smiled at Celestine and Andre. "They won't drown."

Jared knew he was right. Celestine was as driven to pull off her new life as any high school honor student was to get into a great college. Mattu would absorb knowledge in any school. Andre would get his hands and swim with the best of them.

As for Alake, she would be lost with or without Mopsy.

♦

Their own apartment. Where they would build their new lives. A new high school, with the lovely name Free. Where they would be free of everything, including the past and the Finches and their overwhelming kindness.

Kirk Crick explained how to register the donated car.

I am the only driver, thought Mattu.

He, Mattu, was crucial to the family's survival. *He* would fill that car with gas and groceries; *he* would take Celestine to her job and pick her up afterward; *he* would drive Andre to his job, when Andre got hands. And Mattu would get an after-school job in this new town and bring in money.

They would not, however, be free from the threat of the fifth refugee.

We won't get a regular telephone, Mattu decided. A phone means a public listing. A street address in print and online. I'll have a cell phone instead, and that way nobody can find us.

The instant he thought of that, another solution sprang to Mattu's mind. He knew what to do about the diamonds.

Mopsy was the only one of the eight members of this temporary family who wasn't ready. "Norwich is too far away for us to help easily. Alake still needs us."

Kirk Crick brushed this away. "Every school system in the state has a special-ed program. A counselor will deal with Alake. Which reminds me. The apartment building doesn't allow pets."

◆

Alake had never come across the concept of a pet. She would never have believed that grocery stores had an entire aisle for pet food. Now that she had a pet of her own, she could not believe that in this country where people would do anything for you, she could not keep her pet.

Kirk Crick said he would telephone Tay and tell her to come get the puppy.

Life was sweeping forward like a broom, and Alake was rubbish.

She would be rubbish in the Amabo family too. They had been brought together to carry Victor's diamonds. Victor had bought and threatened and killed his way through the veil that tried—and sometimes failed—to protect America from the wrong kind of person.

They didn't call them blood diamonds anymore, because the West was squeamish and didn't like to hear about bloodshed. Americans liked to pretend that bad things weren't really happening. They called them conflict diamonds—as if after a brief argument, shiny stones changed hands. But in Victor's case, Alake thought, these were blood diamonds. And nothing *changed* hands. The hands were cut off.

In a camp with thousands of possible fake daughters, why had Victor chosen Alake?

No doubt because he had once given her an order and she had obeyed. He might need her obedience again. She remembered Victor forcing Mattu to kiss the edge of his machete. Obey me, Victor explained, or end up handless like Andre. People always obeyed Victor.

"Find a different apartment," said Mopsy to Kirk Crick. "Alake loves Jopsy. She needs Jopsy."

"Compared to what they went through, losing a puppy is nothing."

"This is America," said Mopsy. "You get to keep your puppy. That's the point. That's why they came here."

"Puppies are not on the list of reasons to come to America. And the Amabos don't have enough income even for this rundown apartment. They'll have to be subsidized. Once Mattu gets an after-school job and Andre is employed, they'll make it. But they sure won't be buying dog food."

♦

Mattu was not quick with Internet research the way Jared was. It took hours for him to come up with four possible phone numbers. At school, he lied to Mrs. Dowling and pretended he was expected at the guidance office. But Celestine had given him ten dollars in quarters for the pay phones outside the boys' locker room. Jared and Mopsy always checked the caller ID on their phones to find out who was calling before they said anything. If people in Texas had caller ID, they would not know it was Mattu calling and they could not make any connection with a family named Finch.

The first refugee agency Mattu called in Texas listened to his request. But they did not have a refugee named Victor among their current clients. The second agency had no one named Victor. But the third number was answered by somebody who said, "We can do that for you, but wait. First the—"

Mattu hung up. He was sweating with the horror of being a telephone line away from Victor. Even though he'd looked up Texas on a map and used Mr. Finch's ruler to multiply the scale and figure out the number of miles between him and Victor— almost two thousand, which seemed like enough—he was talking to a person who had talked to Victor.

It took hours to calm down.

Then he reexamined his plan.

It was still brilliant.

♦

Victor wasted precious time going in the wrong direction on the wrong turnpikes in places called Pennsylvania and New Jersey. He wasted time sleeping and eating. He was down to only a few days. He used the stolen cell phone from the dead woman's purse to call the New York number. And this time, the dealer answered. Yes, he was in the city. Yes, he remembered the fine diamonds Victor had shown him. Yes, he would pay Victor in cash.

They would meet, he said, at the clock at Grand Central Terminal. It was not safe to transfer gems and cash there. The station would be full of policemen and guards. They would go for a walk together and the transaction would occur elsewhere.

Victor assumed that in such a place he could kill the buyer, keep the diamonds and take the cash.

All he needed now were the diamonds.

◆

On Saturday, donated furniture was rounded up and delivered to the Finches' house. Boxes of donated dishes and pots and microwaves were sorted; Americans always had some amazing extra thing they weren't using. Cleaning materials and canned goods were purchased. These were loaded into a borrowed van, which would sit in the driveway until moving day.

Alake had stayed out of the way. She clung to Jopsy. She prayed that Tay would never come, or that Mopsy would coax Mr. and Mrs. Finch to let Alake keep living here. But of course that was not going to happen, any more than Alake was going to erase her past.

Then it was Sunday, and Emmy Wall did come to church, making too many people for one pew. Mopsy, Mrs. Finch, Emmy Wall, Jared and Mr. Finch sat in a row. And so, for the first time, the four Amabos sat in a separate pew, as if they were a family.

Alake thought that the other three were a family. Mattu was

becoming a son to Celestine and Andre. They needed him, and he was proud and excited to be needed. And he was everything a son should be: tall, handsome, intelligent, athletic. They would form a family and make a home and share a life.

But they would not share it with Alake if they could help it. Celestine's real daughter had been murdered and Alake had been substituted. As if any mother could accept a substitution. At first she'd have to—Kirk Crick and the Finches would check on the Amabos. But they wouldn't check forever—or even for long.

The congregation sang a hymn. The melody was beautiful and the words were sad.

*"Jesus walked this lonesome valley.*
*He had to walk it by himself."*

Alake was frightened by it. Walking by yourself was the worst punishment on earth. The last verse was even worse.

*"You must go and stand your trial.*
*You must stand it by yourself."*

Surely the whole point of Christianity was that you did not have to stand your trial by yourself. God would be there. Why did they sing this horrible hymn that contradicted the Good News?

Because it's true, thought Alake. I have to stand my trial by myself. I have to live with people who hate me. I cannot keep my puppy. I have to walk alone.

Alake had listened so carefully to everything. How to fasten a seat belt. How to use double coupons, a credit card, a vending machine, a revolving door, the Internet.

But what good was any of it, if you had to walk alone?

♦

Jared sat next to his dad on the not-soft-enough cushion of the pew and watched his father not listen and not pray.

Dr. Nickerson's announcements went on and on: a baptism, a wedding, names of the sick, crucial meetings and finally, the joyful news that an apartment had been found for the refugees.

We're all refugees, thought Jared. We all want a safe house. A place with strong walls between us and trouble. My father's two safe houses—home and church—stopped being safe. And now Mom is even making him sit in church with the wife of his enemy. How Christian and how annoying does it get? Jared began laughing silently. "I've decided I kind of like church," he whispered to his father. "It's so crazy."

Dad did not seem cheered by this revelation.

Theirs was not a family or a church that publicly embraced. Occasionally the order of service required people to offer each other the Peace of God. Everybody hated it. You were supposed to hug and get all friendly and everything, but shaking hands was the max for anybody here. Today Jared did something he had never done in church. He put his arm around his father's shoulder and pulled him in tight.

Dad's stiff spine relaxed. His tight shoulders sagged. His set jaw softened. He hugged back.

Jared could not help thinking of Alake, who was never hugged, and perhaps never would be—and who was about to lose the one creature she herself could hug.

They sang a mournful old folk song, not at all Dr. Nickerson's style. Probably some old person's request. It gave Jared a sick feeling, as if it forecast his future. He would walk alone in some lonesome valley.

*"You must go and stand your trial."*

Mrs. Wall sobbed once, out loud, and caught herself.

Was the hymn about court trials, though? Or about everyday trials, like sharing your bedroom or finding diamonds in the ash?

*"Nobody else can do it for you."*

His mother took Mrs. Wall's hand. She had the opposite slogan. Somebody else could always do it for you, or at least with you.

Jared whispered in his father's ear, "What do you bet Mom goes straight from giving refugees a home to escorting wives of felons to court?"

"I'll bet everything I have," his father whispered back, laughing.

♦

"Jesus tells us," said the minister, "that if you have done a good thing for the least of his people, you have done it for him."

I am the least, thought Alake. Every person in this church is better than I am.

Celestine and Andre and Mattu did not know exactly what Alake had done or how often or under what pressure, but it did not matter. She could not be part of the family they were going to make in this town called Norwich, and one day Mattu would put

Alake in his car and drive to some distant place, perhaps even the great void that was New York, open the door and tell her to get out.

At the end of the service, the congregation sang a soft little song to say good-bye to each other.

*"Go now in peace.*
*Never be afraid.*
*God will go with you each hour of every day.*
*Go now in peace, in faith and in love."*

Alake did not know what peace was. There had been none in her life. And faith? What was that? Nothing Alake possessed. But she had been given glimpses of love: the love of this family who had taken her in, the love of this church and the love of her puppy.

*You have to walk it by yourself.*

If I have Jopsy, thought Alake, I can walk anywhere. I have to walk now, before they take my puppy away from me.

In Africa, you could just keep walking and find others who were just walking, and with them, you could sleep by the side of the road and hope for rescue or death. But in America, that did not seem to happen. For Alake to vanish in America, she needed money.

I have a Social Security number, she thought. We all had to get one. Legally I'm too young to work, but at Celestine's job at that motel, half the girls in housekeeping didn't have papers or were too young. I can get a job somewhere and earn money someday. But to take care of Jopsy right now, I have to have money.

Diamonds are money.

# Chapter Thirteen

MONDAY MORNING WAS AS CHAOTIC and confusing as the first day of school, when none of the Amabos had known how to open the sealed carton of orange juice or why the phone rang. Alake held Jopsy tightly. If only she could be in somebody's arms, held this tightly. If only holding something tightly meant that you could actually keep it.

Because Celestine had the privilege of working extra hours that day, Mr. Finch was dropping her off early. They were already gone.

Mrs. Finch was taking Andre to some distant city called Boston for something called a second opinion. She was shouting questions: Did everybody have their homework? Did they have lunch money? Were their cell phones charged? Would Andre please hurry up and get in the car?

Then Mrs. Finch and Andre were gone, and it was Jared shouting. Did everybody have their book bag? We're late, Mattu! You didn't finish your toast, Mopsy. Carry it with you! Alake, put Jopsy in the kitchen and close the door.

The night before, Tay had telephoned Jared. Jared had yelled across the entire house to relay Tay's information to his mother.

"Tay's mom is getting the puppy in the morning," bellowed Jared. "She says leave one of the garage doors up and put the puppy in the kitchen and don't lock the side door, and she'll go in through the garage and get the puppy."

Alake was shattered. Mrs. Finch said, "Say good-bye to Jopsy tonight, Alake. I'm sorry this has to happen, but you've had the puppy such a short time that you won't really miss him. Be my brave girl now."

I don't want to be brave. I want to have Jopsy. And you can love with all your heart even if you've only had your puppy a short time.

Alake had prayed all night long. Let me keep Jopsy, even though I couldn't keep my family or my home or my village or my two teachers or my sister. Please, God.

But here it was Monday morning, and the side door leading from the garage to the kitchen was unlocked and one of the big automatic garage doors was up. Sometime today, Tay's mother would drive into the driveway. She would go into the house, tuck Jopsy under her arm, turn the little knob in the handle to make the side door lock behind her and put Jopsy into her car. She would press the button inside the garage and quickly hop away before the huge heavy door lowered on her, and then she would drive off, leaving an empty house.

And for Alake, an empty heart.

Even Jesus had to walk his lonesome valley by himself. What was this lonesome valley? Was Alake already there? Was it life? Was it America?

"Alake," said Jared, "we're late. Go down the hill with Mopsy."

Alake was holding Jopsy tightly, but not tightly enough. Jared took her puppy away. Jopsy was going to be alone in this house. Nobody wants to be left alone, even puppies, Alake thought.

Especially puppies.

Jared set Jopsy on the kitchen floor. The puppy galloped back to Alake. Gently, Jared shoveled the puppy backward into the kitchen with his huge sneaker and closed the door.

♦

Mattu was in a great mood. He had solved everything. How lucky that he had listened so closely whenever Mrs. Finch taught them something.

That was the great thing about America. Solutions.

In Africa, nobody had a solution to the problems of war and famine and AIDS and drought and mosquitoes and orphans— or if they did, they didn't have the money or the time or the allies to make it work. But in America, as Mrs. Finch demonstrated every day, there was always a solution. Mattu felt so American, so in control. He settled comfortably on the school bus seat. "I meant to ask, Jared. When Erik wasn't in class last week and the teacher got so mad, what was actually happening?"

"Erik skipped. He just didn't feel like school, so he didn't show up. He got in trouble."

"What happened to him?"

"Detention."

Mattu had not known about this aspect of America. "They detained him in a prison camp?"

"No," said Jared, as if any idiot ought to know the meaning of the word "detention." "Erik's on the basketball team, so his punishment is missing practice. For a few days after school he has to sit in the principal's office instead. The whole team hates him now."

Where Mattu came from, punishment was chopping off an arm. He looked out the window of the bus, smiling. This was a great country.

♦

Right after the high school bus left with Alake, Mattu and Jared, the middle school bus arrived at the bottom of Prospect Hill. The middle school wasn't very far. In spring and fall, Mopsy often walked home. But never in her life had she been ready early enough in the morning to walk *to* school.

If I were Alake, thought Mopsy, I'd be kicking and screaming. I should have done that for her. I should have told Kirk Crick where to go. I should have said the puppy is not negotiable.

She was quite proud of this vision of herself talking back to the refugee supervisor.

A few months ago, I would never have thought of telling somebody where to go. I am maturing.

It was time to be called Martha. No more fooling around. She was going to enforce it this time. She'd start with Quinnie.

Mopsy vaulted into her bus, full of plans for acting adult. Nothing could stop her now.

She forgot Alake.

♦

Jared and Mattu were sitting in the back of the bus, where boys always sat, making noise and trouble, while Alake sat in the front, all alone. Nobody else liked being close to the driver, who listened in, and anyway, Alake was not company.

A school bus going in the opposite direction stopped to pick up kids on the other side of the road. All traffic stopped, including Alake's bus.

It was Alake's favorite part of the ride—the obedience of American cars to school buses. All these drivers were exactly like Drew and Kara Finch. They were in a hurry! They had lists! Everything mattered! They must be on time! But never never never would they pass a school bus.

The children climbed onto their bus, waving good-bye to mothers who were waiting with them. Then the mothers waved, the bus driver waved, the safety bar popped back in place and the two buses moved in their opposite directions. It was like television America. But it was real. Happy children, happy moms, happy day at school.

And then there was Alake.

She glimpsed a dog on a leash, which had been hidden by all those people. The mother smiled down at her dog and the dog wagged its tail and the two of them raced up a driveway, the mother laughing and the dog barking.

◆

The high school bus ground to its final stop.

Because he was so tall and because he was sitting by the window, Mattu had a good view of the road. A car coming toward them was not slowing down for the flickering lights all over the bus. It did not obey the stop sign that popped out of the side of the bus. It just kept going. Mattu had never seen a car break this crucial American rule.

He peered down to see what kind of person was driving that lawbreaking car.

◆

One mile past Mopsy's school, Alake's bus stopped at the high school. It was too raw and cold to be leisurely. The kids spurted out of the bus and hurried into the warmth, shouting and laughing, name-calling and showing off, noticing only themselves.

Alake was alone, surrounded by ugly piles of snow shoved off the road by the plows. The once-beautiful snow was black now from car exhaust and sand.

Alake had no books in her backpack. She had dry dog food and a bag of sandwich bread, her Social Security card and a map. She had the timetable for the train to New York, whose station was only four miles away. She had the cash she had stolen from Celestine to use until she could figure out how to use the diamonds.

Alake pulled her hood over her head and her mittens onto her hands. She kept her face down. She was as invisible as a black girl in a white town could be. As soon as a hedge was between her and any peering high school eyes, she broke into a run. She did not know how soon Tay's mother would arrive. Alake would get the puppy and then lock the kitchen door and the garage behind her. Tay's mother would think that Mrs. Finch had forgotten to leave the house open, and she would not call Mrs. Finch to report it, and Alake would have all day. As for Mrs. Finch, she was not coming back till late from the place called Boston.

♦

Mopsy did not go into the school building. She stood in the bitter wind.

I forgot Alake. I didn't comfort her about Jopsy. Mom didn't remember either, because she has so much else to do. I didn't tell Jared to watch out for Alake. What good things are in her life now? thought Mopsy. She has to leave our house and Celestine hasn't ever hugged her. Not once.

The horror of it struck Mopsy forcibly. Alake had to live with people who did not like her.

Mopsy could e-mail Alake, but Alake didn't usually check the computer until she had free time at lunch. And how much comfort was an e-mail, when you got right down to it? Mopsy could phone Jared and tell him to put Alake on. But what good would it do Alake to hear Mopsy's voice? Alake didn't care about voices.

Mopsy wavered.

It was only a mile. She could walk over to the high school—and do what? Say what? In the end, Kirk Crick was right. Alake must swim by herself.

Incredibly, beyond the softball diamond, Mopsy saw Alake running down the sidewalk. Long thin legs pumping. Book bag solid on her back. Heading home.

Mopsy's heart broke. Alake was going to get Jopsy. But then what would she do? Talk Tay's mother out of taking the puppy back? Never happen. Bring the puppy to school? Wouldn't work.

Alake's only choice, really, was to run away.

Mopsy was so not a person who did things without permission. The office would not give her permission to go after Alake. Mom and Dad wouldn't either, if they were around.

But the only thing worse than Alake silent and unloved would be Alake silent and unloved and on the run.

Mopsy didn't have Alake's speed. Twenty steps of running and she was sick of it, so she walked a block. And then another. And another. She gazed up Prospect Hill. When she had a home of her own, it would be in a flat place.

◆

Mattu's heart had not pounded like this since he had run from a machete blade.

*Victor.*

*Here.*

Driving the car that had passed the school bus.

Mattu tried to focus on the high school, the wide halls decorated with banners and art-class projects and retired team jerseys, filled with fat and happy kids, all laughing and talking and yelling and running and so *full* of themselves—was there ever a people so full of themselves!

It wasn't Victor, he told himself.

*But it was Victor.*

I wanted to be safe and believe I had a solution and I could make everything all right and the bad things would go away. I'm as childish as Mopsy—I, who know evil.

He had to tell somebody in authority that Victor was here.

But nobody would believe him. This town did not have people like Victor, and nobody here really believed in evil or that evil people routinely did evil things. They would say, No, no, Mattu, that was in Africa. This is here.

But they wouldn't really believe that it happened in Africa either.

If it was Victor in that car, the only possible outcome was violence. Mattu would be responsible for not having told the authorities. They would send Mattu back to Africa and the refugee camp. He would never have the new high school called Free and the new apartment with Andre and Celestine and would never be the driver of their own car.

But realistically, who could Mattu tell?

The friendly middle-aged officer whose beat was the high school? The fat old guy whose patrol car was generally parked near one of the three red lights? They didn't know any more about real trouble than the Finches.

Then Mattu realized why Celestine had been so fierce when she had insisted that if Victor tried to follow Mattu, Mattu must never come back. It wasn't to save herself, or Andre.

It was to save the Finches.

The American family was far more at risk than the Africans. When you wanted to terrify or harm people—which was all Victor did—you started with the weak. Americans knew nothing of pain or fear. They were not strong like Mattu and Andre and Celestine. They could not withstand what Victor threw at them.

Victor would know this.

The father would not get home till late this evening, so the person whose job it was to defend the family was not here to do it. But even if Mr. Finch were here—or if something horrible took place so that Victor waited for him—Victor would not go after the father. He would go after the father's weakness.

Usually that would be the children. But Mattu thought the weakest one in this family was the mother, Kara. The one who believed she could control everything and handle any problem. Kara did not know how to handle a Victor.

But a Victor could always handle a Kara.

Mattu thanked God that Kara Finch and Andre had taken their long drive to the distant city.

Alake was the unknown. Body and soul, Alake was stretching

toward being an ordinary person. She could never do it, not with her past. Alake's weakness would be her puppy.

But of course, Victor had not come to kill the Finches, find Alake or deal with puppies. He had come for his diamonds.

The timing could not have been worse.

It's all right for the moment, thought Mattu. The house is empty. I can telephone everybody in the family and tell them to stay away. Then somehow I'll explain to the police who and what Victor is.

Mattu was ill with the list of things he had done wrong. "Jared," he whispered.

"Not now, okay? I didn't finish my calculus."

Mattu tugged on his sleeve. "This is more important."

Jared shook him off. "Not to me," he said irritably, walking away.

# CHAPTER FOURTEEN

ALAKE WAS HALFWAY UP PROSPECT HILL when she heard a car behind her. There were so few houses up here that every driver would recognize her and know that she ought to be in school. Alake veered behind the wide, dark branches of a massive hemlock. She hoped it wasn't Tay's mother. As soon as the car passed, she raced on up the hill, legs trembling, lungs weakening.

The car did pull into the Finches' driveway. It was a beautiful car, long and sleek, with none of the filth from snow and road salt that usually coated cars here. How could she solve this? Couldn't God have given her even ten minutes to—

The driver of the shiny car stepped out.

For days now, maybe weeks, Alake had forgotten. Even in her terrible dreams and even in the constant memories in which Victor starred, Alake had forgotten that Victor was alive and in America.

How amazing that his sponsors had given him such a fine vehicle.

Alake caught herself. She was turning into Mopsy. Nobody had *given* that car to Victor.

The garage door was still open, so Tay's mother had not gotten here after all. But the empty open garage shouted that no one was home. Victor surveyed the house for a moment. He did not look behind him, which was good, because Alake was out on the road, entirely visible, and had nowhere to retreat. Victor walked swiftly into the shadows of the open garage. Alake dropped to a crouch and scuttled behind a small leafless bush. Victor's hand would be reaching toward the unlocked kitchen door. On the other side, he would find Jopsy. Victor and Alake did not come from a part of the world where dogs were loved. A dog was something to kick or kill.

Alake had failed to keep her sister safe, and her teachers, and her parents, and everybody else on this earth. She still had a chance to keep her puppy safe.

Victor wanted his diamonds and Alake knew where they were. In exchange for the diamonds, would Victor drive Alake and Jopsy to New York? Because New York was where he had to go; it was where the diamond buyers were. Would he agree to let Alake out somewhere in that vast city and then drive on, never to cross her path again? She knew Victor. He would promise anything and shoot anyway.

The puppy had already learned that when a door opened (as it always did, if you waited long enough), speed was crucial to avoid capture. Victor must have opened the door, because Jopsy hurtled out of the garage and scrabbled on the frozen ground. How excited he was from his successful escape and the fresh air!

Keep running! Alake thought at him.

And of course, he did. Following his nose, Jopsy kept running right to Alake. And when he found her, he barked for joy.

◆

Wow, did Tay's mother drive a nice car! Mopsy was impressed. And Mopsy's timing was pretty good—maybe she could negotiate puppy-visiting rights. Did the church volunteer exist who would haul Alake back and forth to see a dog?

Mopsy crossed the cement floor of the garage, silent in her thick-soled sneakers, and walked into the kitchen.

A man was holding Alake by her face, his fingers gripping her chin and mouth and nose as if Alake were a football. In his other hand he held a gun.

Mopsy had never seen a gun except on television.

The man threw Alake away like a piece of firewood. She hit the wall so hard that the watercolor hanging there fell off its nail. The glass over the painting smashed, and shards scattered all over Alake and the floor.

The man smiled.

Now Mopsy knew what the Amabos had been afraid of, why they dreaded the sound of a door opening or a phone ringing. This person.

The puppy whined for attention.

The man aimed a kick, but Alake intercepted and took the kick. The kick made a sound, or perhaps Alake's ribs made the sound. But Alake remained silent. She scooped Jopsy into her arms and rolled away.

"It's okay," said Mopsy quickly. "He's just a puppy. He can't hurt you."

The man faced her. He clicked his gun in a way that did not cause it to shoot but made it even more frightening. Mopsy iced over. She couldn't think through the frigid fear.

"Where is Mattu?" The man's accent was thick and draggy, like Celestine's and Andre's.

"He's at school," said Mopsy. She forced a thought out of her paralyzed brain. "You want the diamonds, don't you?"

He and the open hole of his gun stared at her. "You know about the diamonds?"

"Mattu doesn't know that I know. I was peeking in his boxes."

"Show me."

Alake will run away the minute we head upstairs, thought Mopsy, so she'll be safe. Once he's counting his diamonds, I'll race downstairs too. As soon as I'm outside, I'll dig out my cell phone and call 911.

The man gestured to her to go first. When she walked by, he yanked off the backpack that held her cell phone and flung it across the room. He nodded an order at Alake, who fell in line behind Mopsy so that they formed a little parade—Mopsy first, then Alake and the puppy and then the man.

The treads seemed high. The carpet felt rough. Her sneakers snagged and she stumbled. It took forever to reach Jared's room. Her brother's side was messy. Mattu's side was beautifully arranged, so he could gaze upon his new possessions in rows and pairs.

On the dormer shelf sat the two Tupperware containers.

"The cardboard boxes fell apart," explained Mopsy. "Mom

gave Mattu plastic boxes instead." The seal would be tight. The man couldn't hold the gun and open the boxes at the same time. That would be her chance.

But he made Mopsy open them.

The instant she lifted one, she knew she was in trouble. It was way too light.

She pried it open, knowing already that the diamonds and the ashes were gone.

♦

Could Jared just be done with the refugees' problems and their needs and their noise? Could Mattu just shut up already? "Oh, please," snapped Jared. "Stop it with your torture stories. If Victor is so important, why didn't you mention him before?" Jared felt sufficiently hostile toward Mattu to belt him. If Dad felt this way, no wonder he left before dawn and came back after midnight every day.

"I was scared," said Mattu. "I misunderstood things, Jared. I thought somehow we were safe. I pretended that, anyway. But no one is safe. You must not let anybody in your family return to the house."

"You thought you saw this guy in a car," said Jared. "Like you can recognize someone in a speeding car, Mattu!"

"I know Victor. It was him, Jared. He has found the right town. Perhaps through the Internet. Or perhaps just phone calls to the right resettlement agency. Soon he will find the right house. Call everyone in your family. They must not go home."

"Fine. Whatever." Jared flipped open his cell. He hit Mopsy's number first. I better not have a roommate when I get to college, he thought. I can't handle it. I like distance.

◆

Broken glass fell off Alake's jacket as she walked. On the carpet of Jared's room, the shards glittered more brightly than rough diamonds would.

Alake was just as shattered as that glass. How could Mopsy be home? American children were always where they were supposed to be. They did not wander. They obeyed the incredible number of rules about where to be when. Mopsy should be safe in school.

Jopsy barked, wanting to get down and celebrate all the fine people in his life.

Alake gripped the puppy tightly. Her fingers hurt, but not from holding her dog.

She had tried never to touch the machinery in this household. These people had machines to brush their teeth and cook their food and clean their floors and write their letters. The only machine Alake had touched in her previous life had been an assault weapon. Her fingers still felt it. Even now, if she touched something cold, like a fork, she would feel the metal where Victor had told her to pull.

Now her soul and her hopes were as cold as her fingers.

Don't ask me to hold the gun, she thought. Don't ask me to do the shooting.

Victor flung the blue containers around. Then he flung Mopsy. "Where are the diamonds?" he shouted.

Mopsy lay crumpled on the floor.

Alake neither moved nor spoke.

But Victor always knew a person's weakness, and he knew this time, too. He said to Mopsy, "Want to know who Alake is? She's a killer. A child soldier. One of mine."

If only Alake could have denied this.

"She stood there," said Victor, "and watched while her parents were killed. She murdered her own teachers. She watched while her sister was killed. Then she joined me."

And that was all true, in a way. And now Mopsy knew the terrible thing Andre and Celestine knew, and she too would avoid Alake and hope not to be contaminated by her.

"Don't be silly," said Mopsy, in that amazing American way; the absolute refusal to believe people were wicked. Mopsy staggered to her feet.

Victor tried again. "Her name isn't Alake, either. Nobody you took in is really named Amabo. I substituted them for a family I killed when the real Amabos did not cooperate." He smiled at this memory. He had lost yet another tooth. Alake had seen enough American smiles now to know that Americans were made deeply anxious by bad teeth. She was not surprised that Mopsy seemed more upset by Victor's rotting teeth than by his gun.

Alake had often thought of what she would say when she started to talk. Lovely things. Warm and thankful things. But no. That was not to be. She would speak to survive. She used English, their common language. The loving words she had tried so hard to get out of her mouth for so long had not yet come, but the terrible words came quite easily. "I will get you the diamonds," she told Victor. "Then you take me and my puppy to New York and leave us there." Alake did not look at Mopsy. The moments of friendship and kindness were in the past.

Mopsy gasped. She too had expected Alake's first words to be something else.

"You know where the diamonds are?" said Victor.

"I took the diamonds. I came here to get my puppy and then I was going to get the diamonds and leave."

Victor laughed. "So you were the strong one after all." He studied her thoughtfully. "This will work. The police are looking for me, but they won't be looking for a father and his daughter and a dog."

Alake did not ask why the police in America were looking for Victor. She could guess. "The diamonds are not in the house," she said. "In this house, they snoop."

"That's what she said," agreed Victor, aiming his gun at Mopsy.

"I will not give you the diamonds if you hurt her," said Alake. "We will go in your car. We must drive."

Victor shrugged and shoved Mopsy down the stairs and out of the house. He and Alake both knew he would just hurt Mopsy after he got the diamonds instead of now.

Alake said, "The puppy might bark. We will leave him in the kitchen."

"We're not coming back. You want the dog, you bring the dog."

They climbed into the beautiful car. Alake directed Victor down the hill, through the village and into the bleak marina, full of boats but empty of people.

◆

Jared was exasperated.

Mopsy had promised Jared to keep her cell charged and on. Had she forgotten? Or was she sitting in class, not daring to answer?

"What's this about, anyway, Mattu?" Jared demanded. "Summarize it. One word. Don't run on about torture and warlords. I can't stand it."

"Diamonds," said Mattu.

◆

Wind whipped the blue plastic sheets covering hundreds of boats. Flagpole ropes rattled like bad drummers. Mopsy was squashed in the front seat between Victor and Alake. She was so frightened that she was not even having thoughts; she was all fear.

"Here," said Alake.

Victor stopped the car and got out, dragging Mopsy after him. Alake shut Jopsy in the car. It began to sleet. Mopsy hated sleet. It was like failed, angry snow.

Salt water or not, the harbor was frozen around the edges. The open water was the color of stones and death. The wind was brutal, slicing like knives through Mopsy's lungs.

◆

"There was a fifth refugee on our plane," said Mattu. "Victor. The diamonds are his."

Jared felt like some old-fashioned machine, gears slowly moving into place. "And Victor would be . . . ?"

"The man who spilled the blood that made them blood diamonds."

Blood like Andre's. From chopping off hands.

Blood diamonds, not conflict diamonds.

I knew there was danger, thought Jared. That's why I told Mopsy to keep her phone with her. What am I, insane? You don't ask an eleven-year-old to handle her own danger!

Jared flipped his cell open and hit 411. "Keep talking," he ordered Mattu.

"Victor thought a family of four would be less suspicious and we could smuggle his diamonds more easily than he could. Diamonds cast no shadow in X-ray machines, you see, so it is not likely that they will be found unless the person carrying them makes the authorities suspicious."

"Prospect Hill, Connecticut," Jared told the automated voice. "River Middle School."

"We expected to land in New York City," said Mattu, "and then Victor would take the diamonds and go. We four would find our own housing and jobs. But that did not happen. I thought we were free of him. I thought we had disappeared into this little town. But Victor is here. I saw him."

"You kept some killer's property in my house, when you knew that killer would show up to claim it?" said Jared. The phone company was willing to make the connection at no charge if he pressed one. Jared pressed one. "Hi, it's Jared Finch. I need to talk to my sister, Martha. She's in Mrs. Jackson's sixth grade."

Daniel appeared in the hallway, walking toward them with that leisurely, always prepared, exception-to-the-rule manner he had, rather like Tay. Jared grabbed Daniel's arm. Daniel stared at Jared's fingers trespassing on his arm. He gave Jared a warning look. "What do you mean, Mopsy didn't come to school today?" Jared shouted into his phone. What was happening? How could Mopsy not be in school? He disconnected. "Daniel—you drive to school today?" demanded Jared.

"I drive to school every day."

"I need your car." Jared hustled Daniel down the hall. Mattu followed, which Jared figured was a good thing, because Jared was going to run him over after he'd made sure Mopsy was safe. "You drive, Daniel," ordered Jared. "We're in a major hurry." He dialed his house. Nobody answered.

The blood diamond guy will go to our house, not the middle

school, he thought. He understood a hundred things halfway now. The Amabos had come as refugees but also as screens for a smuggler. They had actually thought that the trees and rocks and curving country roads of Connecticut were shelter from a killer who had only to pick up a phone or open a Web site and find them.

Find *us*, thought Jared.

Mattu began explaining Victor to Daniel, who turned out to be a slow, careful driver. Jared didn't even think Daniel was a teenage boy; he was some old coot who couldn't see thirty feet away. "Faster!" he shouted. "Go through the light!"

Daniel came to a full stop, looked both ways and waited for the green.

"Victor will be armed," said Mattu.

Daniel took his foot off the accelerator. "What do you mean, armed?"

"That's him!" shouted Mattu, pointing at a gleaming black Lexus that was turning off the tiny main street and heading down the marina lane. "Mopsy's with him. And Alake!"

"Are you sure?" asked Jared. How could a refugee end up with a new Lexus? Jared went from completely worried to completely skeptical.

The marina was an unlikely destination for anybody this time of year, let alone an African smuggler, if this even was Victor, and anyway, how could Victor have located Mopsy? As for Alake, she was in school. She'd gotten on the bus *first*. Jared *knew* she was at school. "Step on it!" he said to Daniel, just in case.

Daniel was not a stepping-on-it kind of driver. He was a

creeping-along kind of driver. Plus he was driving with one hand, and with his other hand—actually, with his other thumb—he was dialing 911 on *his* cell phone. "Police," Daniel said calmly. "Marina Road. An assault in progress." He said to Mattu, "You better be right. I'm going to be really annoyed if I've cut school and called the police and it isn't about anything."

♦

Alake walked out onto the breakwater.

Mopsy could not believe it. Alake had refused even to get near that breakwater when they'd been here before.

The rocks were slick with ice. Thick half-frozen water bumped up against them. If Alake lost her balance, she'd slide into deep frigid water under a lid of slush.

Twenty steps out, Alake fell. Mopsy screamed.

The man hit Mopsy. "Shut up."

Mopsy shut up. My face is broken, she thought. He broke my face.

Alake caught the rim of a rock and did not fall into the water. She crawled on instead of walking. She did not look back at Mopsy or the man.

Was this the Alake who had been inactive to the point of being comatose? Mopsy marveled. Had that same Alake taken the diamonds, put them in a Ziploc bag or something and sneaked down to the waterfront? Had she dropped this bag into one of the holes created where the mortar had crumbled?

It might have looked like a perfect hiding place—a deserted marina in the middle of winter—but the sea would have eaten the bottom out. The hole would go all the way through. The diamonds were probably long gone, sucked out by a violent tide.

A fierce gust of wind tossed slush onto Alake's face and arms. There was no sign that she noticed. She kept going.

So a person thinking about diamonds thought of nothing else.

I don't know Alake after all, thought Mopsy. I made her up to fit what I wanted in a sister.

Victor was breathing hard. His eyes were glued to Alake.

Victor is wrong that nobody will know he's masquerading as a father with a daughter and a puppy, thought Mopsy. I'll know. I'll tell the police everything. I even memorized the license plate number.

Victor glanced back at Mopsy, realized she was dawdling and grabbed her by the face, the way he had grabbed Alake in the kitchen.

Mopsy saw how true it was, that she was young for her age. Victor would not leave her alive to tell.

◆

Alake was only a few feet from the end of the rocks when she found the hole. A narrow chink, just wide enough for a hand. She swallowed her terror of the icy unknown and stuck her arm down.

She felt nothing. She pulled her arm back out and shifted

position, sliding hideously closer to the edge. The water slurped eagerly. Wind like a jackal's teeth bit her wet arm. She tried from another angle.

"I've found the box!" she shouted. "But it's frozen to the bottom. I can't get it free." She put her eye to the hole. "Your arm is longer."

◆

"You first," Victor told Mopsy, letting go of her face.

Mopsy knew how deep the water was. If Mopsy slid off, she would drown in her own town at her own beach while her own personal refugee looked for diamonds.

Alake, who was not Alake.

Because Victor had killed the real one.

Mopsy dropped to a crawl. Victor didn't do anything because he was struggling with his own balance. He dropped the gun in his pocket to have both hands free.

Alake crouched over her diamond hole, scrabbling for what mattered.

◆

Three people were out on the breakwater. Jared saw them clearly.

The man Mattu said was Victor.

Alake.

And Mopsy.

What could they be doing there? What could they possibly want out there? What kind of insanity—

Jared leaped out of Daniel's car, screaming and waving.

The man called Victor turned to look. He put his hand in his pocket. There was something athletic about his stance—a sort of readiness to make a play. His hand, when he withdrew it from his pocket, looked oddly lengthy.

*He will be armed*, Mattu had said.

◆

Alake stood up.

Jared was running toward them, ice or no ice.

But bullets travel faster than humans.

Victor could kill Mopsy. He could kill Jared. He could hit Mattu and Daniel. He could do it in moments. It was his skill.

Alake's plan had not yet failed. She could still carry it out.

Alake thought about her family, these Americans who had welcomed her and asked for nothing in return. She thought about God, and there was time to pray.

Let me be good, just once. Let me atone.

She thought about the poem Tay had read, with its promises to keep.

She had not had time to make promises, but she would keep them anyway.

She stepped forward.

She wrapped her arms around Victor and flung herself side-
ways into the sea, taking Victor with her.

♦

The sound of sirens filled the air.

Daniel shouted into his cell phone, guiding the police.

Jared gathered his bleeding little sister in his arms.

Mattu caught up.

But where Alake and Victor had been, there was nothing, not
even a hole in the slush. Invisible waves beneath the icy lid of
winter had already closed it up.

In the end, *Alake* had been the precious gem.

Alake had been willing to lay down her life. Silent, unloved
Alake, who had had but one taste of joy—a few days with a
puppy—calmly, and without fanfare, had given her life for her
friends.

Jared was such an American. Built into the soul of Americans
was the desire to help. They didn't always help wisely or well, but
they did always leap into the water to try.

"You hold on to Mopsy," said Jared fiercely to Mattu. "No
matter what, you keep my sister safe." Jared slid into the water. It
was so cold he couldn't open his eyes; so cold he was out of air and
strength in one heartbeat.

I'm going to die, thought Jared, and he knew just how stupid
he had been, hurling himself into ice water, when one of his goals
in life was Don't be stupid.

His flailing arm hit stone. The breakwater. He braced his feet against it and flung his arms outward, searching the slushy water.

*God!* he prayed, which was all he had time for. He felt something soft and closed his hand on it.

The cold paralyzed him. He could not pull himself or it to the surface.

*God.*

A particle of strength returned. Jared kicked upward.

Whose body do I have? he thought. What if I have the killer and not Alake?

◆

Dull, careful Daniel was also an Eagle Scout who kept valuable things like rope in the trunk of his car. He made a large loop, tossed it to Jared and was hauling him up as the police cars arrived. To Mattu, Daniel said, "You explain this to the police. I'll back up whatever you say. Certainly *I* don't know what's going on. You got secrets to keep, Mattu, this would probably be the time to keep them."

They put Mopsy in the first ambulance.

They stripped Jared's wet clothes off and popped him on a stretcher next to his sister.

They put the survivor in the second ambulance.

They had to wait a while for a third ambulance, but that was all right, because the dead are good at waiting.

◆

They didn't keep Mopsy in the hospital, just pumped her full of antibiotics and gave her codeine for the cuts and bruises, then sent her home. Mopsy slept and slept, and when she awoke the first time, her mother and father were sitting by her bed, and nothing that had happened in her house or out on the breakwater seemed possible or real. When she woke up the second time, Celestine was there.

Mopsy said sleepily, "So who is everybody, really?"

Celestine seemed puzzled. "We are Amabos. We met that man Victor on the plane, you know, and were afraid of him. Here, look what I have for you. A bowl of ice cream, nice and soft, just the way you like it."

Mopsy sat up.

"I have just come back from our new apartment," said Celestine, who had always been good at changing the subject. "It was small and dirty, but the church volunteers scrubbed while I was at work, and now the apartment is still small, but it is very clean."

Mopsy took the ice cream. "You know what, Celestine? I'll miss you."

◆

When Mattu finally cornered Jared, his host wouldn't look at him. Mattu didn't like looking at himself either.

"What are you going to tell people?" Mattu asked Jared.

"What did *you* tell them?"

"Lies." Without the lies, Mattu was afraid they would be deported.

Jared sighed. Finally he said, "You had good reasons to come to America. I think you should've done everything differently, but you didn't, and maybe you couldn't, and Mopsy's okay, and tomorrow you'll have what you came for. A new life."

How American, thought Mattu, to move on like that. And how Christian—to accept and forgive.

Mattu had come to the conclusion that most Americans were extraordinarily Christian, even when they weren't Christian by label. They all believed in that great rule: help your neighbor.

Alake had helped the most of all. She had never had the diamonds, of course. Mattu himself had taken the diamonds. Once she realized the containers were empty, Alake had had only a few seconds to figure out how to destroy Victor without weapons. She had drawn him out to sea.

Lord, prayed Mattu, forgive me. She is the one who put our American family first. Save her, Lord.

He looked around Jared's room for the last time. Then he looked at Jared, who was still glaring at him. "Thank you for sharing your room," said Mattu softly.

◆

Jared said nothing. He followed Mattu downstairs and out to the driveway. It was snowing very lightly, although it seemed too warm for snow, and the air felt thick and soft and lacy.

Mrs. Lane was supervising in the driveway, shouting orders to donors and packers. She beamed at Jared. "Isn't it wonderful that we've all worked so hard and accomplished so much all these weeks! I'm so proud of my contribution."

Jared was not aware that she had done any work whatsoever. His mother had done every bit of it, except for the driving. He caught up to Mattu. "One thing you haven't told me, Mattu. Where are the diamonds now?" He felt morally superior because he'd put his diamond back. "You kept them for yourself, didn't you?"

Mattu shook his head. "I had to get them back to Victor. But Victor doesn't leave people alive. So I went online, located refugee agencies in Texas, where George Neville said he was going, and asked each one if I mailed them a package, would they get it to their client Victor? Two of them said they didn't have a client named Victor. But the third agency said they could. So on Sunday, I sneaked into your father's office and took a padded envelope. I poured the ashes into the fireplace and the diamonds into the envelope. Then I took the same amount of stamps that your mother put on her package the day we had our post office lesson. I addressed it to the agency in Austin. I didn't put a return address on the envelope, because then Victor would know where it came from. I thought I was being very clever."

You were, thought Jared. If I were Mopsy, I'd clap. You learned about a thousand things to pull that off.

What would they do, these people in Texas, when they opened the package addressed to Victor, the refugee who had murdered their supervisor? Would they see gravel and throw it away? Or recognize diamonds and sell them for a good cause—or for greed? Or turn the package over to the police, where it might lie unopened in some evidence box? "The postmark shows part of the zip code, though," he said, finding it difficult to get out of teaching mode. "They're going to put two and two together and know it came from you, what with all the publicity and the police."

Mattu shook his head. "When Mrs. Kara took Andre to Boston for his second opinion, Andre hid the package under his shirt and mailed it there."

Jared was filled with admiration. Just escaping his mother's vigilance would have been a task and a half, but also hiding stuff from her and finding a mailbox? "Good plan," said Jared.

"No. A terrible plan. We did nothing right. We kept dangerous secrets. We are still keeping the secrets, but they are not dangerous now."

"You never wanted to keep the diamonds?" Jared asked.

Mattu shook his head. "They were in the shadow of evil."

Jared's scalp prickled. Now he knew four people in the world who knew that money is not treasure. Love is treasure. Food and hands and a roof of your own are treasure.

Mrs. Lane gave permission to the first van of donated stuff to set out for the new apartment. Jared and Mattu waved. The second van drove off. Jared and Mattu waved.

"Is Celestine your mother?" asked Jared.

"No. But she and Andre are married. They had kids. The kids are dead. I don't know about Alake's family."

"Hop in, you two," said Mom, backing her car out of the garage and pausing next to them. "I'm dropping Andre at the apartment and we'll give everything a final check."

All the mysteries are cleared up, thought Jared. But not all the work is done. There is one more thing.

◆

Alake was in a white room with white sheets and a white table and a white wall.

People were kind. Mrs. Finch had come to give her a hug and a kiss. Tay came, and Jared, and Alake tried to find words to thank them, but no words entered or left her mouth. It was as if her only speech had been with Victor, and that would last forever. Alake would never talk to nice people, only evil ones.

Get-well cards and flowers came from school and church.

Alake shivered under the blankets.

The concussion from when her skull had hit the stones of the breakwater was healing.

But everything else was broken open. People would have pieced the truth together now. They would put Alake in some pen like that corner of the refugee camp. The hymn would come true after all: she would have to walk this lonesome valley by herself.

Better not to try walking at all. Better to sink back into what she had been: nothing.

When the door of her hospital room opened this time, it was

not an aide, a doctor or a nurse. It was Celestine, who hated Alake for being alive when her real daughter was not.

Go away, thought Alake.

But Celestine sat on the bed. She took Alake's limp hand. How often in America people had held Alake's hand—that distant extension of Alake, which had once pulled a trigger.

"They know nothing," said Celestine. "When Mopsy repeated what Victor told her about us, I laughed and said it was nonsense. They believed me, of course. Americans always want to believe that evil is nonsense."

The Finches did not know what Alake was? Mopsy did not understand? The Finches still thought she was Alake?

"We have moved into the new apartment," said Celestine. "It is empty without a daughter. You saved the daughter of those who saved us. That makes you my daughter now. Come home. From our new home, you will go to school again, and make me even more proud than I am now." Celestine pulled Alake into her arms, her black African arms, with the scent and the grip and the warmth that Alake had once known, and Celestine rocked her. Celestine's fingers moved over the stubble of Alake's hair, caressing her cheeks and feeling her throat, as a mother does, to be sure that all is well.

A terrible sob came out of Alake's throat and terrible tears burst out of her eyes.

They rocked together, weeping for things past and things that might come true.

The door opened again.

Alake did not want an interruption. It was wonderful to hold a puppy, but infinitely more wonderful to be held by your mother.

In came Mopsy and Mrs. Finch, then Andre and Mr. Finch. They were all smiling.

"We're here to check you out of the hospital," said Mopsy, dancing around. "The doctor says you can come home. Not our home this time. *Your* home. That apartment is not perfect, Alake. You don't even have your own bedroom. You're going to sleep on this thing called a futon. By day it's a couch, and at night it's your bed in the living room."

A mother is enough, Alake told herself. And a couch in the living room is enough. I can't ask for more.

But she was already an American. She wanted more.

And more came.

Because Americans believed that if there was any chance you could have it all, you should have it all.

Jared walked in, grinning. Mattu came in behind him, wearing an exceptionally large ski jacket. Two people could have stood inside that jacket.

Alake was so glad to see them. So amazed that Mattu would bother.

"I talked to the landlord," said Jared. "Mom was right, you know, Alake. TV publicity does a lot for people. Daniel not only called the police, he called the TV station, and they had a camera there before Victor's body even got dragged out of the water. There was all this coverage of how you saved Mopsy's life and stuff. I found the landlord and I said to him, 'So Alake needs her puppy.' And do you know what the landlord said, Alake?"

Mattu unzipped his jacket. A small brown and white muzzle appeared, and huge brown eyes.

"The landlord said, 'You bet.' He saw on TV what you did and he said, 'A heroine like that gets to have her puppy.'"

Mattu poured Jopsy onto Alake's bed and Jopsy poured love all over Alake. When she wept for joy, Jopsy licked the tears. Alake could speak no words, but she found them in her heart.

Thank you, God, for families.

◆

The family named Amabo finished the paperwork to check their daughter, Alake, out of the hospital.

The family named Finch took the elevator to the ground floor and went out to their two cars.

"Why don't I drive the Amabos back to their apartment?" said Jared's mom. "You three can head on home."

"Good idea," said his dad, always grateful not to have to schlep anybody or anything anywhere. "Want a driving lesson on the way home, Jared?"

Jared was always ready for a driving lesson. He put his arm, however, around the sister who had not turned out to be so annoying after all. "Want to come, Martha? You can sit in the back and be jealous, because it'll be years before you get to drive."

"But I'm very mature for my age," said Martha Finch, smiling.

"I bet I pass the driver's test while you're still trying to learn parallel parking, Jared."

He didn't argue. He was kind of a slow learner at important stuff. But he was a lucky guy. He came from a family of good teachers.

# A NOTE
# FROM THE AUTHOR

A church where I was once organist runs its own refugee ministry. I belong to the Congregational Church, sometimes called the United Church of Christ. Many of our Connecticut churches have sponsored refugees. The ministry owns a multifamily house, where refugees live when they first arrive. Over a three-year period, this church has welcomed eighty-seven people from ten countries.

My own church was asked to take in a family of four African Muslims from Sierra Leone. They lived with me for the first month, but this is *not* their story. This book is fiction. Nobody in this book represents a real person. To ensure that I did not accidentally use the name of a real refugee, I even made up the last name Amabo (it's Latin: "I will love") and the first names Mattu and Alake. The Refugee Aid Society is a fictional group. Prospect Hill is a fictional town.

Mrs. Finch was correct—most of us hear and know very little about Africa.

In 2004, there were more than three million refugees in Africa. How can we even start to think about that many people? How can we picture any of them?

I was privileged to know a refugee family, but not everyone can do that. I recommend a wonderful coffee-table book called *Hungry Planet*, by Faith D'Aluisio, with amazing photographs by Peter Menzel. It won a James Beard Foundation Award. Its stunning pictures show what families in locations all over the world—from an African refugee camp to a farm in Ecuador and a city in Mongolia—have for dinner and how they get it.

Although I have statistics about Liberia and Sierra Leone from sources like the United Nations and Church World Service, it's *Hungry Planet* I want you to look at, so I'm using a few statistics from that book.

### About Darfur
### (a region of Sudan in Africa, at this writing in the midst of war)

Number of refugee camps: 160+

Percentage of Darfur's population living in these camps: 30

Percentage of those people who saw a family member killed: 61

### About Chad
### (a neighboring African country)

Number of camps for Darfur refugees: 11

Number of refugees in one camp: 30,000+

Main food for a family of refugees for one week: 39 pounds of sorghum (a grain). It isn't ground into flour; that must be done by hand.

Years of warfare since 1960: 35

Percentage of houses *with* electricity: 2

Doctors for every 100,000 people: 3

What are we to do to help this desperate continent?
So far, no long-term solutions are being offered.
Perhaps the person who figures out how to help will be you.

**CAROLINE B. COONEY** is the author of many books for young people, including *A Friend at Midnight; Hit the Road; Code Orange; The Girl Who Invented Romance; Family Reunion; Goddess of Yesterday; The Ransom of Mercy Carter; Tune In Anytime; Burning Up; The Face on the Milk Carton* (an IRA-CBC Children's Choice Book) and its companions, *Whatever Happened to Janie?* and *The Voice on the Radio* (each of them an ALA Best Book for Young Adults), as well as *What Janie Found; What Child Is This?* (an ALA Best Book for Young Adults); *Driver's Ed* (an ALA Best Book for Young Adults and a *Booklist* Editors' Choice); *Among Friends; Twenty Pageants Later;* and the Time Travel Quartet: *Both Sides of Time, Out of Time, Prisoner of Time,* and *For All Time.*

Caroline B. Cooney lives in Madison, Connecticut, and New York City.

# Another unforgettable reading experience from Caroline B. Cooney

Lily will rescue her younger brother Micheal after their father abandons him in an airport—but will she be able to rescue herself from the bitterness and anger she feels?

Available in bookstores and from online retailers.